Frog Face and the Three Boys

Frog Face and the Three Boys

DON TREMBATH

THE BLACK BELT SERIES

ORCA BOOK PUBLISHERS

Canadian Cataloguing in Publication Data
Trembath, Don, 1963-
Frog Face and the three boys

ISBN 1-55143-165-3

I. Title.
PS8589.R392F76 2000   jC813'.54   C00-910885-8
PZ7.T71925Fr 2000

First published in the United States, 2001

Library of Congress Catalog Card Number: 00-107319

Orca Book Publishers gratefully acknowledges the support for our
publishing programs provided by the following agencies: The
Government of Canada through the Book Publishing Industry
Development Program (BPIDP), The Canada Council for the Arts,
and the British Columbia Arts Council.

Cover illustration by Dean Griffiths
Cover design by Christine Toller
Printed and bound in Canada

IN CANADA:	IN THE UNITED STATES:
Orca Book Publishers	**Orca Book Publishers**
PO Box 5626, Station B	PO Box 468
Victoria, BC Canada	Custer, WA USA
V8R 6S4	98240-0468

03 02 01 • 5 4 3 2

To my friend, Bob Turow, who taught me everything I need to know about tiger kicks, which isn't much, and Manual, who actually did teach me karate, although you wouldn't know it.

1.

The three boys sitting in the office were not friends with one another. They were not talking. They were waiting for the principal to arrive.

The boy closest to the door was Jeffrey Stewart, or Stewie, to the few people in the school who bothered to call him anything.

He was small and soft and turned pink in the face at the slightest hint of stress or embarrassment.

He had been sent to the office by his grade seven teacher, Ms. Rudy, a tall, pinched woman with piercing eyes and a nose as sharp as a beak. She had decided to turn the last half hour of the day into a spelling bee, and Jeffrey had refused to participate.

The word given to him had been "salamander," an easy one, really, compared to some of the others, but Jeffrey, a new boy to the school, and in the throes of yet another anxiety attack, had turned shocking pink, stood motionless and said nothing.

Ms. Rudy had given him two warnings. Then she had pointed to the door, her finger as stiff and severe as a knife blade, and he had left the room.

Sitting next to him in the office, noisily unwrapping an *Oh Henry* bar, was the hefty bulk of twelve-year-old Charlie Cairns. Charlie was still in his gym clothes — navy blue shorts and a plain white T-shirt, black socks and rarely used running shoes. He had been sent to the office by his gym teacher, a lean, sinewy, spark plug of a man named Mr. Roper.

Charlie's crime had been turning the regular cross-country run across the fields and through the streets of the quiet little town of Emville, Alberta, into a mid-afternoon walk to the store for some snacks.

"Do you know how important your health is to your future, young man?" Mr. Roper had said by way of a lecture to Charlie, when the boy finally returned to the gym. "Do you know that of all the courses you will take throughout your education, none will matter to you more as an adult than your health, which is exactly what physical education is about? Do you know that?"

"Yes, I do, sir," said Charlie, showing complete and total respect.

"And yet, still you neglect yourself as if you didn't care."

"It's my blood sugar, sir."

"Don't lie to me, Charlie."

"I wish I was, sir."

"There's nothing wrong with your blood sugar levels. You're not diabetic."

"If you only knew the whole story, sir."

"Take it to the office, boy."

"Can I stop for a chocolate bar? My head's still a bit fuzzy."

"Get out of here."

Rounding out the threesome was Sidney Martin. He was sitting next to Charlie.

Sidney's T-shirt was torn at the collar and the knuckles on his right hand were scraped and sore. There was a small mark near his left eye. The scalp beneath his brush cut was still glowing red from energy and anger.

He had been sent to the office after getting into another fight with his nemesis, Matt Thompson, who had made fun of Sidney's bicycle.

"New wheels there, Sid?" Thompson had said, standing by the bike rack with his friends.

"Bite me," said Sidney, his anger starting to flare.

Twenty years ago, kids Sidney's age would have turned their noses at the sight of his ten-speed bike, which looked at least that old. Today, it was a bona fide relic.

"Easy, little fella," Thompson had said. "Your mommy's not here to throw punches for you."

That had been enough. Sidney, who was not a particularly big kid, but whose every ounce of flesh on his body seemed to be made of lean muscle, charged Matt with the speed and ferocity of a pit bull terrier.

The fight had been a short one: a couple of stiff pokes by Thompson, and three quick rights by Sidney, who, although he gave away pounds and inches to his enemy, was still more than capable of holding his own.

"You're a dead man," Matt had shouted as Mr. Bryson, the Shop teacher, lifted Sidney away.

"Not before you," Sidney had shouted back.

Matt Thompson was given a warning for his role in the fight. Sidney, who clipped Mr. Bryson with a stray punch as he struggled to break free, was hustled down to the seat he was currently occupying.

The three boys sat in silence for several

more minutes, then the short, round figure and bulging eyes of Mr. Duncan, the principal, blew in through the door.

To many people in the school, Mr. Duncan looked like a frog. Today, he looked like a frog on a mission. An exciting mission.

"Gentlemen!" he said, his face beaming as he walked behind his desk. "So glad you came by for a visit."

"Always a pleasure, sir," said Charlie, who, along with Sidney, knew Mr. Duncan quite well.

"And you've waited so patiently. My, my. You must really want to see me. Good afternoon, Sidney. Another scuffle, I see. And Charlie. Mr. Roper tells me you got lost along your way this afternoon. Everyone else went left to the ravine, and you went right to the 7-Eleven store."

"It's a Winks store, actually, sir," said Charlie, to clarify.

"Don't trouble me with fine details, my friend. I'm not really this jolly. I'm just pretending."

"I understand, sir," said Charlie.

"Good," said Mr. Duncan. "And you," he went on, looking now at Jeffrey, "your teacher tells me that you need to spend some time in the counselor's office. Something about your extreme shyness getting in the way of your ability to learn. Any truth to that?"

Jeffrey's face began to glow.

"Good heavens. You *are* a meek one, aren't you," said Mr. Duncan.

Jeffrey said nothing.

"Well, my friends, I think I have the solution to all your problems right up here in my head."

"I knew we could count on you, sir," said Charlie.

"It's a clever idea, it takes place right here at the school, and it works. And I know it works, because it worked for someone in my very own family." Mr. Duncan moved around to the front of his desk and sat on the top of it. "But before I tell you what it is, let me ask you something. Does anyone here know who Morris Duncan is?"

Sidney nodded without enthusiasm.

"Of course, sir," said Charlie. "He's your son."

"That's right. He's my son. My oldest son. And what a fine boy he is. Bright. Clever. Athletic. Intelligent."

"Words my mother can only dream of using about me one day," said Charlie.

"Right now, Morris is down at Michigan

State University on a football scholarship. Word is, he has the potential to go in the first round of the National Football League draft next year as a wide receiver. Of course, he might also go to Harvard to pursue his master's and doctoral degrees in medicine."

"You and Mrs. Duncan must be very proud," said Charlie.

"Oh, we are," said Mr. Duncan.

"Would you shut up?" said Sidney, turning to Charlie.

"Yes, Charlie," said Mr. Duncan, with patience. "Would you mind?"

"Not at all, sir," said Charlie, who did not return Sidney's glare.

Jeffrey stayed out of the exchange completely.

"Now let me ask you this," said Mr. Duncan, moving on with his story. "Have any of you ever heard of Willie Duncan?"

Sidney let out an impatient sigh and rolled his eyes and shook his head. Jeffrey remained motionless.

"Sounds like a pickpocket to me," said Charlie. "Or a jewel thief. The notorious Willie Duncan. I'll look it up in one of my dad's history books when I get home. He loves that kind of stuff."

"Willie Duncan is my other son," said Mr. Duncan, ignoring Charlie. "He's three years younger than Morris."

"Oh, Willie," said Charlie, slapping himself on the forehead. "I thought you said Billie. Oh, I know Willie. He's a great kid."

"Willie did not have the high-profile up-bringing that my son Morris did. He was not the first student from Emville to bring home seven gold medals from the provincial track and field championships. He did not represent his school at the Canadian Science Fair in Toronto. He was not invited to New York to sit in on a session of the United Nations on the strength of an essay he wrote on world unity."

"Sounds a lot like me," said Charlie.

"You say one more word ..." said Sidney, pointing a threatening finger at Charlie.

Mr. Duncan held up his hand to silence his listeners, then carried on with his story.

"Willie was at home during all of those times learning his alphabet, learning how the multiplication tables worked, learning how to read. Everything that came easily to Morris came with great difficulty to Willie. Everything. Then one day, about seven, eight years ago, he came home from school and asked his mother if he could take karate lessons. A karate instructor had visited his school and talked up the benefits of karate and so on. Willie had never asked us anything like this before. So we checked it out and said okay, and off he went, starting with two times a week, then three times, and finally, as he worked toward his black belt, four and five and six times a week."

"Wow," said Charlie, in awe.

"Today, he is a second-degree black belt and an associate instructor at the Moran School of Karate right here in town. Not to mention an honors student in engineering at the University of Alberta."

"I think I read about him in *Chicken Soup for the Young Man's Soul*," said Charlie.

Sidney turned and belted Charlie hard on his right shoulder.

"Ouch!" said Charlie.

"I told you to shut up," said Sidney.

"Boys! Cut it out," said Mr. Duncan, sounding immediately like a regular principal.

Jeffrey's face turned a deeper shade of pink after the outburst.

Charlie rubbed his shoulder.

"Now, I tell you this story for one reason," said Mr. Duncan once peace had been restored. "What Willie lacked in his life, whether it was order, confidence, the ability to deliver a devastating roundhouse kick with either foot, I don't know, but whatever it was that he lacked, he found it in karate. And now he is a teacher, except they don't call themselves teachers, they call themselves something else. I can't remember what the word is. But now he is a teacher, and he has been given a beginner class to run all on his own, his very first one, and it starts tonight. And I am sure he would be very happy if three of his first students came from his old school."

"I'll start looking for someone right away, sir," said Charlie, still rubbing his shoulder.

"That won't be necessary, Charlie," said Mr. Duncan.

"Are you an idiot?" said Sidney, looking with disdain at the fat boy beside him.

"The classes start at 6:00 and run for ten weeks. They're taught right here in the school gymnasium. They go for one hour. I've telephoned your parents. They all seem pleased with the idea. Membership is free, since we're letting them have the gym this time around for nothing."

"Don't you think a week of detentions would do the trick?" said Charlie.

Mr. Duncan smiled.

"I am a man of vision, Charlie. I see great potential in the three of you, but there are obstacles in your way. Perhaps a few hours at karate will remove them for you the way they did for Willie. Besides, tell me what staying after school for an hour would do for the three of you. You'd fill your face with food from the cafeteria. Sidney would probably get into a fight with somebody. And Jeffrey here would sit by himself in the corner. You would all be home late from school. I'd have to talk with all of your parents. The teachers who'd have to stay would be mad at me. And what would you gain from it? Nothing. You go spend some time at karate. There, you will learn things."

Charlie began to squirm slightly in his seat. Physical activity of any kind was not his favorite way of passing the time.

"Tonight is usually the night I read to the elderly, sir," he said.

"Your mother failed to mention that."

"She's one of them, sir. Her memory is gonzo. Right out the window."

"I'll see that someone takes your place," said Mr. Duncan. "Anything else?" He looked in turn at the three boys: Jeffrey was starting to quiver visibly in his chair; Charlie had a second bead of sweat rolling down the side of his

2.

Charlie was the first of the threesome to arrive back at the school. His mother drove him to the front doors, stopped the car and said briskly, "Out you go. I'll be back at seven to pick you up."

She was showing him no pity.

He didn't deserve any, or so she said. Besides, she had added, over supper, that dimwit of a principal had finally come up with a good idea, and she did not want to be the one to stand in the way of it.

Charlie's mother, Bella Cairns, was a big woman with silvery gray hair piled high on her head like a rain cloud, and a laugh that sounded to most people like a thunder clap. She and Charlie's father, her husband, Ray, a truck driver with a belly that hung over his belt like a sack of cement, had four daughters and one son. The girls were all older than Charlie.

"You think it's a good idea? What happens if I get hurt? What if someone hits me?" said Charlie, as he ate more potatoes.

"What if?" said his mom. "Maybe you will get hit. Maybe you'll get kicked. Maybe then you'll learn to take the easy way out and run through the damn ravine like that little pipsqueak Roper wants you to."

It was a habit of Mrs. Cairns to provide a one- or two-word description of the people she was talking about, and it was rarely a flattering one.

"You can hit back too, you know, Charlie," she had said, her tone softening a bit as she saw the fear flood into her son's face. "You're a big boy. It's about time you learned how to handle yourself."

He was still feeling scared as he stepped out of the car and watched his mom pull away. He was wearing his gym clothes again. He had a sweater over his arm, but it was a mild night and it was only mid-September, so he would not need anything more to wear.

He walked into the school and down the familiar hallway toward the gymnasium. The school was quiet. Outside, kids were playing soccer and football and there were people out riding their bikes and jogging and walking their dogs. But inside, Charlie heard practically nothing, save for the thumping of his own anxious heart.

The gym doors were open when he arrived, but the gym itself was empty. Charlie walked in and looked around. He had been on this floor a million times since he began attending J. Cooper Elementary School in grade one. Now he was in grade seven, the king of the heap, as it were, and he was as nervous as a tiny first grader who had never been alone in a school before.

He heard the outside door of the school open and close and then footsteps coming toward the gym. Charlie tried to look nonchalant and relaxed, but his eyes kept darting toward the door.

A young man walked in. He was short and squat in a powerful, broad-shouldered way, and he wore glasses that just covered his large, protruding eyes.

"Good evening," the young man said, taking a look at Charlie. He had a friendly voice and a thin, sincere smile. "You're here for the karate?"

"I sure am," said Charlie, feeling instantly better now that he was talking to someone. "You must be Willie."

"That is exactly who I am," said the young man, switching on the lights in the boys' and girls' locker rooms. "And from the looks of you, you must be Charlie."

Charlie grinned. Good old Mr. Duncan must have had a talk with his son.

"I am indeed," said Charlie, extending his hand for a handshake. "Nice to meet you, Willie. You'll have to go easy on my hand here. I just got the cast off it a week ago."

"Oh, no," said Willie, preparing for the worst. His dad had warned him about this kid.

"The doctor said I shouldn't even be here tonight."

A look of mild concern and amusement passed across Willie's face. "What did you do?"

"I busted it this summer," said Charlie, assuming the demeanor of a streetwise kid. "I was helping the old man unload his rig and a sack of concrete fell on top of it."

"Ouch," said Willie.

"Two months I had to wear the stupid thing."

"Two months?" said Willie, taking a closer look at Charlie's right hand. "You can't even tell. It's as tanned and thick as the other one."

Charlie shrugged. "I'm a fast healer. Plus I've broken so many bones before. This finger.

This thumb. My foot. Two of my ribs."

"You must play pretty hard," said Willie.

"I get my nose dirty."

"Dad said you didn't like the physical stuff. He said that's why you're here."

Charlie made a face. "He said I *don't* like the physical stuff?"

"That's what he said."

"It's my mom who doesn't like the physical stuff."

"Maybe that was it."

"The way she sees it, every time I do something physical I break another bone. She said no way when I told her about coming here. She figured I'd break my whole body in half in a class like karate. I had to tell her I'd take it easy."

"Good idea," said Willie.

"Well, it's not my first choice, but sometimes you have to compromise," said Charlie.

"Absolutely."

"Ordinarily, I'd be going full bore in here already."

"I bet."

"But something is better than nothing, I guess."

"That's right."

"I had to promise her, though, no sparring."

"Oh-oh."

"Absolutely no sparring," said Charlie, holding up both hands in front of him to emphasize the point. "She'd lay an egg right on the spot if she came in here and saw me going at it with somebody. And she'll come in. She said she's going to, and I know she will."

Willie stopped to think for a moment. "Well, we don't really spar too much at the start," he said, making like he was trying to work through Charlie's predicament. "It's pretty much just stretching and learning the techniques. We do some punching and kicking, but not at anyone. It's just in the air, so you learn how to do it."

"All right," said Charlie, nodding, and thinking. "That sounds okay. I can't see her having a problem with that."

"Most people are okay with it," said Willie.

"So there's no contact at all," said Charlie, to clarify.

"That's right."

"Just punching the air and pretending."

"That's sort of what we do."

"That sounds okay."

"I mean, there's contact in some of the things we do, but there's definitely no sparring for the first little while."

"That's good," said Charlie, feeling immeasurably better. "Mom'll like that."

"I'll make sure I clear it with her before we get to the hard stuff," said Willie reassuringly.

Charlie waved him off. "I'll tell her myself. If you say it the wrong way, you'll lose her. You'd never see me in here again."

"Then you tell her," said Willie, and Charlie nodded as if to say, not a problem, it's taken care of, as Willie knew it would be.

After their conversation, Willie ducked into the locker room to change. Three other boys arrived for the class. Then two girls walked in. They were both tall and slim and giggling. One had long, dark brown hair and a floppy red sun hat pulled down low over her eyes. She had a bright smile and freckles all over her face. The other girl was shorter by a pair of inches and wore glasses. Her hair was sandy blonde and long past her shoulders.

They went straight into the girls' locker room to change.

Then Sidney walked in. He was wearing a tight white T-shirt and gray sweats that had been cut off just above the knees. He entered the gym and saw Charlie. Charlie smiled and nodded and waved him over. Sidney didn't move. Nor did he return the nod or the wave, so Charlie walked over to him.

"Hey, buddy," said Charlie, with a big smile on his face.

"Knock it off," said Sidney, looking around the gym.

"Hey, you can relax. I checked him out. He's okay," said Charlie.

"What?"

"Willie. I checked him out. I got here early so I could meet him. See what he's about. He's okay. He's all right."

Sidney gave Charlie a look. "You think I was worried about what kind of a guy Willie Duncan is?"

Charlie shrugged and continued to glance around the gym, as if he was sharing information of tremendous importance. "I'm just telling you. He's okay. He checks out. He's one of those CMU guys."

Sidney continued to glare. He was not in the mood for Charlie and his little games. "What's a CMU guy?"

"Can't Measure Up to his big brother. Don't you watch Jerry Springer? They had a whole show on it. Little brothers who can't measure up to their successful, older brothers. They had all these families on the show beating on each other because they hated each other's guts."

Sidney took in a deep breath and shook his head. "Charlie, do me a favor and go stand over there," he said, pointing to the far corner of the gym.

"What for?" said Charlie, looking surprised.

"Just do it. Go stand over there."

"What for? I'm just telling you something you should know about."

"Because I'm going to hit you, that's what for, and if I do that again, I'm going to get in trouble. So go stand over there."

"I'm standing right here," said Charlie, holding his ground. "Why would you want to hit me? I'm helping you out."

"Then how about this," said Sidney. "When we get into sparring, you're my partner, all right? Don't go running around looking for the little girls. Don't go picking on somebody the size of your leg. Stand where you are, and wait for me to arrive, because you are my partner."

"All right," said Charlie. "But we won't be doing any sparring for a long time."

"How do you know?"

"I asked him."

"What'd he say?"

"He said, 'We won't be doing any sparring for a long time.' I asked him why and he told me not to ask him anymore."

Sidney thought about that for a second. "I thought you said he was a good guy."

"He is. He just has a sore spot about sparring, I guess. Maybe he got beat up or something. But don't ask him about it. He got really mad."

Sidney stared at Charlie for another second, then he shook his head and moved away to the far corner of the gym.

3.

The class started at 6:00 sharp. It did not go particularly well.

Willie Duncan, looking even more powerful and imposing in his karate uniform, called a *gi* around the world by fellow students of karate, tried right off the bat to instill the respect, discipline, and protocol that the study of any martial art is famous for, but the seven kids in his class were really not quite ready for it.

He stepped out of the change room, fully attired in his white top and pants, black belt, and bare feet, and bowed to the room before him. He then approached the students, who were all just hanging around in different parts of the gym, and called them together and bowed to them.

"Thank you, my teacher," said Charlie, bowing back with reverence, as if receiving communion. The rest of the class just looked at him, until Willie told them to bow as well.

He took a quick attendance, noting only that Jeffrey Stewart had failed to show up for class, and then went over some of the terms he thought they should be familiar with. For example, during karate classes, the gymnasium they were practicing in was to be called a *dojo*, and, as their instructor, he was to be addressed as *Sensei*, pronounced sen-say, Duncan.

"Can you spell that for me, please?" interrupted Charlie. "I'm keeping a journal of all this, and I'd really like to get the words right."

"I'll give you a handout," said Willie, who was already tiring of Charlie and his mouth.

"I'll give him a hand out, too," said Sidney, clenching his fist, which led to a lecture from Willie on the nature of karate, and the respect with which each maneuver and technique should be regarded, and the danger involved should that respect be ignored.

"*Shomen hajiki*," he said, extending his right hand in front of the class, his fingers held tightly together to form a shape as lethal and sharp as the head of a spear. "Fingertip strikes. You get one of these in the Adam's apple and it can kill you. *Hiji tsuki*. Elbow strikes. One of these in the nose, and your face will look like a tomato that's been smashed against the wall."

"Cool," said one of the other boys in the class, a tall gangly redhead named Mason.

"How do you do that elbow thing again?" said Sidney, already practicing.

"Never mind," said Willie sternly. "I'm just telling you. These aren't things you go and show your friends at school. You use them when you have to defend yourself, and when you're here. And you'll be in big trouble with me if I hear about you using karate to pick a fight with somebody. That's not what we're here for."

"I know how to do a roundhouse kick," said the girl with the brown hair and freckles and the floppy red sun hat that she had tossed into a corner of the gym when the class started. Her name was Joanne, but as she said during attendance, everybody called her Joey. "My brother showed me."

"Let's see it," said Sidney, looking skeptical.

"No," said Sensei Duncan, shaking his head. "No roundhouse kicks."

"Come on," said Sidney. "She's a girl. How much can it hurt?"

"Oh, please," said Joey's friend, Samantha, looking at Sidney in disgust.

"Oh, please yourself," said Sidney. Then he

turned toward Joey and said, "Come on. Let's see it," and before Sensei Duncan could say anything else about the dangers of practicing for real, Joey stepped forward and swung her right leg up as if to kick Sidney square in the face, and then pivoted at the last moment so that her kicking foot swung around and caught him flush on the side of the head, right on the temple, with her stiff, pointed toes.

Sidney went down as if clobbered with a wrench, and grabbed the side of his head.

Mason, the tall redhead, and Charlie, along with the others, gawked in astonishment at Sidney lying on the floor.

"That was awesome," said Mason, breaking the temporary silence.

"Very impressive," said Charlie, nodding in agreement. He looked up at Joey and smiled. "Pass on my regards to your brother."

"You should have kicked the little creep harder," said Samantha.

Sensei Duncan glanced down at Sidney, then over to Joey and said, "We usually just kick to the shoulders when we're practicing."

"Oh," said Joey.

"So no one gets hurt," said Sensei.

"He's not hurt," said Samantha. "He's embarrassed."

Sidney pulled himself up into a sitting position. He was still rubbing the side of his head, and blinking more than usual, and working his jaw muscles to see if they were still able to move.

"Are you hurt?" said Sensei, kneeling down to Sidney's level.

Sidney shook his head.

"Do you believe me now when I say we have to be careful with what we learn here?"

"Will you ever challenge a girl to kick you again?" said Samantha, who seemed to be enjoying Sidney's pain more than anyone.

"Sidney, my friend," said Charlie, changing the subject, "I think I know how you can put an end to your enemy Matt Thompson once and for all."

Sidney glanced up at Charlie and nodded his head. He had been thinking the same thing. Forget the elbow strikes. The roundhouse kick was now the first maneuver he wanted to perfect.

Charlie, however, had a different idea. "Just get Joey here to fight him for you. One fancy kick to his coconut and he'll be crying like a baby."

Sidney turned and glared at Charlie once again. Then Sensei Duncan rose to his feet and said, "All right. Let's get this class back on track. Line up for *jumbi undo*. Warm-up exercises."

When he was initially handed his first class to teach, Willie was told by Sensei Moran, the founder of the Moran School of Karate, not to expect too much from his students. "They're beginners," Sensei Moran had said. "They'll want to learn everything in the first day, and they'll have no idea what they're doing. Just be patient with them. Have fun."

It was advice that Willie had come to class with every intention of heeding, but halfway through *jumbi undo*, which was really just a basic collection of loosening-up exercises, he decided that he could not. From Charlie complaining that the floor was too cold for his feet, to Sidney pestering him about doing more kicking, to Samantha telling Sidney to shut his mouth, this small group of seven innocent kids had gotten to him.

"No more talking," he finally said with authority, his big eyes glowing with anger. "This is a karate class. When I talk, you don't talk. When I tell you to do something, you do it. If you don't know how to do it, you try it anyway. You don't complain. You don't stand there and do nothing. You don't tell me what to do. And you don't tell anyone else what to do. You stand there and you look at me and you watch me. You do as I say, and do as I do. I run the class. Not you. I am your sensei. And you better figure that out."

After a moment or two of silence, Charlie raised his hand. "Very well put, Sensei," he said, adding a bow at the end.

"Charlie, you shut your mouth," said Sensei Duncan, pointing his finger for emphasis. "I've had it with you."

"Now you're starting to sound like Mr. Campbell in mathematics," said Charlie.

"I don't care who I sound like. Any more from you and you're out."

"That would be really awful, sir."

"No," said Willie, walking toward Charlie. "That's what you want, isn't it? I'll put you up here instead, at the front of the class, and you and Joey can practice your roundhouse kicks on each other. How would you like that?"

"I pulled my groin last week, sir. It's still a little tender."

Willie shook his head. "You tell a lie every time you open your mouth, don't you?"

"Not every time," said Charlie.

"And that was another one," said Willie.

"No, it wasn't."

"Yes, it was."

"No, it wasn't."

"Are you sure?"

"Absolutely."

"You better be sure."

Charlie nodded. "I'm sure." It had not been his intention to provoke a master martial artist into a confrontation on their first day of classes together, but he had, and he was quickly regretting it.

Fortunately for him, Willie Duncan was thinking along much the same lines. It had not been his intention to lose his cool so early into his career as a karate instructor.

"So don't tell any more of them, okay?" said Willie, his voice softening but his message just as clear.

"I'll do my best," said Charlie truthfully.

Willie turned away and went back to the front of the group. They practiced *sokuto geri*, side snap kicks, and *shomen geri*, front kicks, until the class came to an end. Everyone did their bows. Willie thanked them for coming and said he looked forward to seeing them all again on Thursday.

He was fully aware that he was telling a lie of his own, but under the circumstances, he could not have cared less.

4.

At school the next day, Jeffrey Stewart was called down to the office and asked by Mr. Duncan to explain why he hadn't been at karate the night before.

At the tone of Mr. Duncan's voice, and the directness of the question, and the look in his eye, Jeffrey turned hot pink in the face and started to squirm in his chair and even, for a second, had to remind himself how to breathe, but Mr. Duncan did not let him go until he got his answer.

"I'm not going anywhere, Jeffrey," he said. He was sitting behind his desk this time, his arms crossed in front of him, his face stern and unwavering. "And neither are you."

"My grandpa didn't want me to go," said Jeffrey, finally, staring down at his knees.

"Your what?"

"My grandpa."

"Your grandpa?"

"Yes. My grandpa."

"Your grandpa didn't want you to go."

"That's right."

Mr. Duncan stared at Jeffrey for a moment. "What does your grandpa have to do with any of this? I am your principal. I talked with your mother. We both thought it was a worthwhile idea."

Jeffrey took a deep breath and looked up at Mr. Duncan, who was now leaning over his desk, waiting for the answer. "My grandpa said that little Dougie Duncan was not about to tell him what he should do with his grandson."

"What?"

"He used to know you when you were a little boy. You used to come into his store with your mom. He said you used to cry all the time because you nicked your finger on a saw blade once and you were always afraid of doing it again."

Mr. Duncan continued to stare at Jeffrey for another moment, then he sat back in his chair. Two times he started to say something, then didn't. Finally, on the third time, he said, "Who is your grandfather?"

"Sam Anderson."

"Sam Anderson?"

"Yes. Sam Anderson."

"Old Sam Anderson?"

Jeffrey shrugged. "He is now, I guess."

"He was old fifty years ago when I was going into his store with my mom."

Jeffrey shrugged again. Fifty years ago was before his time.

"How old is he now?" said Mr. Duncan.

"He turned eighty-seven last May."

Mr. Duncan shook his head. "How's his health?"

"Good. He still rides his bike to buy a paper every morning."

A look of reflection passed across Mr. Duncan's face. He remembered a bicycle always parked outside the old man's store. "That's funny your grandpa remembers that. I was just thinking about it the other day myself."

"He said you cried more than any other kid he ever met."

Mr. Duncan smiled. "Well, if the truth be told, *he* was the one who nicked my finger on the saw blade. He said, 'Here, young fella. Touch this. See how sharp it is.' And he moved it a little bit just as I touched it and he cut my finger. So I was scared of *him* every time I went into his store, not the saw blades."

"Well, he just remembers you crying all the time about something."

Mr. Duncan sat back in his chair. This was not the first time he had experienced the constraints of working in the same town he'd grown up in, but he had never encountered anything quite like this.

"So what exactly did he say?" he said.

"Just what I told you," said Jeffrey.

"And why is he being consulted about any of this when I already talked with your mother?"

"Because we live with him now. My mom and I moved in with my grandpa and grandma this summer, after the divorce."

Mr. Duncan very briefly closed his eyes and took in a deeper-than-usual breath. "And he said, in spite of the fact that I am your principal and I told you to do something, and also in spite of the fact that your very own mother endorsed the idea, that you shouldn't go to karate, and so you stayed home."

"Yes," said Jeffrey.

Mr. Duncan smiled again, but it was not a very nice smile.

"Well, Jeffrey, on Thursday night, you be at karate, or I will take a less creative and more punitive approach to dealing with your situation, okay? And if your grandfather has a problem with that, please invite him to ride his bike over here, and we'll talk about it."

Jeffrey gulped and said nothing, but he could not see this news going over well with his old Grandpa Anderson, who had referred to Mr. Douglas Duncan as a "sissy" as a boy, and a "big sissy" now.

"You can go now," said Mr. Duncan.

Jeffrey stayed seated.

Mr. Duncan began writing something on a sheet of paper, then he looked back up at the boy sitting before him. "I said you can go now."

Jeffrey squirmed slightly in his seat. "That's not the only reason I didn't go," he said.

"I beg your pardon?"

"That's not the only reason I didn't go."

Mr. Duncan put down his pen. It was a very important form he was filling out, but for the moment it would have to wait. Again.

"What is the other reason, Jeffrey?" he said, with growing impatience.

"My grandmother doesn't want me associating with Charlie Cairns or Sidney Martin."

"Say that again."

"My grandmother doesn't want me associating with Charlie Cairns or Sidney Martin."

"Did she say why?"

"Yes."

"What did she say?"

"She said Charlie's whole family are a bunch of bigmouths and Sidney's mom is a thief."

Mr. Duncan stared at Jeffrey for a moment, then he closed his eyes again, this time for a longer period of time than the first. His frustration with this whole little arrangement was starting to get to him. Nevertheless, he decided to be diplomatic. "Well, Charlie does have a big mouth, there's no questioning that. And he uses it very well. I can't speak to the claim that Sidney's mother is a thief."

"She stole money from my grandpa."

"She what?"

"She stole money from my grandpa."

"When?"

"Twenty-three years ago. She was in his store and he bent down to get something from behind the counter and her and her friends grabbed some money out of the till and took off with it. He phoned the police, but because he didn't know which girl actually took the money, they couldn't charge them. But he was sure it was Tizzy."

"Tizzy?"

"That's Sidney's mom."

"Oh, yes. So it is."

"My grandpa said he'd never forget her."

"Apparently not," said Mr. Duncan.

"And Grandma said anyone who steals money out of their pocket is not going to become a family friend."

"I don't blame her," said Mr. Duncan.

"She wants the police to re-open the file."

"I think that's very unlikely."

"I do, too. But Grandma seems to think it's possible. She's going down to the station tomorrow."

Mr. Duncan took in another deep breath and put down his pen. What had started out as a terrific idea was now becoming quite the chore to carry out. "Well, Jeffrey, I can appreciate your grandparents' concerns, and certainly their knowledge of the community and the people who live here is as deeply rooted as anyone's I can imagine. But the fact of the matter is, you and Charlie and Sidney all happened to show up in my office at the same time, and it was the combination of the three of you and your respective situations that made me think of karate in the first place, and I am not going to let go of my idea just because of a little resistance from your elders. Do you know what I'm saying?"

"Not really."

"I'm saying, be at karate on Thursday night

at 6:00, or I will start getting angry. And I don't like getting angry. I get angry when I get angry, and I don't like that. So go. I'm not telling you to make friends with the other boys. I'm telling you to go to karate. It's part of this new way of dealing with things that I'm trying to establish here. Do you read me now?"

"Yes," said Jeffrey. He knew when enough was enough, and for Mr. Duncan, enough was enough right now.

"You know what I'm saying?"

"Yes."

"And so you'll be at karate Thursday night?"

"Yes."

"Good for you."

"Thank you, Mr. Duncan."

"You're welcome, Jeffrey."

"And Mr. Duncan?"

"Yes, Jeffrey?"

"Should my grandpa make an appointment to see you, or just come by when he has the chance?"

Mr. Duncan stared at Jeffrey one more time. He had been this close to making a clean break with the kid, and now this. "Tell him to make an appointment."

"Okay, Mr. Duncan. Thank you," said Jeffrey, and he slipped out of the office.

5.

On Thursday night, just as he said he would, Jeffrey went to karate.

His mother was working the late shift at the library and his grandfather had fallen asleep watching the news, so he walked from his home to the school on his own.

"You be careful," his grandma called to him as he left. She was still not in favor of the idea, nor was his grandpa.

"I will."

"And put your hat on."

Jeffrey turned around. "It's warm out, Grandma."

"I don't care. You put your hat on. I gave you a hat, you put it on."

"All right," said Jeffrey, and he dug reluctantly into his coat pocket and put his hat on.

"And you tell that Tizzy Martin's boy we

want our money back," she said, as he hit the sidewalk.

"Okay."

"With interest! Twenty-three years!" she called after him.

He kept walking. He had no intention of saying anything to Sidney about money, but he knew better than to say anything like that to his grandma. She could be just as crusty as his grandpa when she wanted to be, and Jeffrey had a feeling she wanted to be right now.

When he arrived at the school, he slipped quietly into the gym and waited for the class to begin.

He took his shoes and socks off when he saw the other kids standing around in bare feet.

He was content to be by himself, and to stand with his back to the wall and not say a word to anyone until it was time to start.

That was the way Jeffrey did most things, and he was not about to change now.

Then he saw Charlie coming toward him.

"Hey, Peewee," said Charlie, looking troubled. "I got trouble."

Jeffrey said nothing.

"Son of Frog Man over there says we're going to do a little sparring tonight, and Sidney wants me to be his partner so he can tear my head off and use it as a pillow on his bed."

Jeffrey started to turn pink in the face at the sound of the word sparring. It was a polite way of saying fighting, and he wanted nothing to do with it. "Why?" was all he managed to say.

"Why? Because Sidney's a deranged little psychotic who needs blood on his hands to survive. I don't know why. I must have said something to cheese him off."

"That's hard to believe," said Jeffrey, who, in spite of his shyness, actually had a sarcastic sense of humor.

"Hey," said Charlie, pointing a finger. "Don't get smart. You can get hurt in here, too, you know."

"I'm not getting smart," said Jeffrey.

"Well, you should be. You're gonna need something to survive in here," said Charlie. Then he added, out loud but to himself, "Where's a good broken-bone story when you need one."

"A what?" said Jeffrey.

"Nothing. I'm just thinking to myself. On Monday I told Willie I'd broken my hand and pulled a groin muscle. I shouldn't have used both of those at once like that."

"You keep track of your lies?" said Jeffrey.

Charlie gave him a look. "They're not lies. It's fiction. I'm going to be a writer when I grow up. My Language Arts teacher told me to practice every chance I get."

Jeffrey rolled his eyes and said nothing.

Charlie went back to looking troubled and thinking about his most recent predicament. Then Joey walked into the dojo with her floppy red sun hat pulled snugly over her head, and her friend Samantha beside her. Joey smiled and waved at Charlie.

"Who are they?" said Jeffrey, surprised to see girls in a karate class.

"That's the girl who kicked Sidney in the head Monday night."

"The what?" said Jeffrey. He hadn't heard the story before.

"The girl who kicked Sidney in the head. Laid him out like a sleeping bag right over there."

"When?" said Jeffrey, but Charlie didn't answer. Jeffrey turned to look at him and saw that the troubled look on his face had disappeared. In its place was a small, sly smile.

"You okay?" said Jeffrey.

Charlie turned and looked at him. "I will be," he said. Then he left to talk with Sidney.

He found him in the corner of the gym with the heavy bag, punching it so hard he let out a grunt every time one of his flying fists thudded against the thick black leather hide of the bag. Beads of sweat glistened on his forehead and dropped down along his nose or rolled onto his cheeks. The knuckles on both his hands were scraped raw.

He looked like a lightweight prizefighter training for his shot at the title.

Charlie walked over to him and tapped him on the shoulder. Sidney stopped punching and turned around. "What?" he said harshly, as the sweat washed over his face. He did not like being interrupted.

"I'm just here for a second," said Charlie, holding up his hands defensively. "I'm just here to tell you something."

Sidney waited for a moment, then he said, "What is it?"

Charlie put his hands down. Then he asked a question. "How's your head, anyway?"

"My what?"

"Your head," said Charlie, pointing to his own temple. "Where she kicked you."

"It's fine," said Sidney.

"No headaches or anything like that?"

"No."

"No swelling?"

"No."

"Blurred vision?"

"What do you want?" said Sidney, with mounting impatience.

"I'm just here to say hi," said Charlie.

"Hi," said Sidney. "Now get lost."

"And to tell you that everything's been taken care of."

"What?"

"And to tell you that everything's been taken care of."

A look of confusion passed across Sidney's face.

"What 'everything's' been taken care of? What are you talking about?"

"Your head?" said Charlie.

"What about it?"

"And Joey, the girl who kicked you?"

"What about her?"

"And the sparring we're gonna do tonight?"

"What about it?"

"It's taken care of."

"What is?" said Sidney.

"All of it," said Charlie.

Sidney moved toward Charlie until their noses were practically touching. "Tell me what you're talking about, Fat Boy, or I give this heavy bag here a break, and start working on you."

Charlie raised his hands again and took a step backwards. "I'm not here to cause trouble," he said. "I'm here as a friend. Now you're a tough guy, right? I'm not. You have a reputation to protect. I don't. You were floored by Joey with one flick of her foot. I've got enough blubber on me to withstand a thousand kicks to almost any part of my body. So, I'm going to spar with her. Not you. You stay here with your heavy bag, and when Willie Boy calls us to attention, you go stand beside Jeffrey or Samantha and you can play with them. I'll take the heat for you."

Sidney fixed his eyes on Charlie. "Say all that again."

"No one will ever know about our little arrangement," said Charlie. "I'll even put on an act like I don't want to do it. Like I don't want to be her partner. But I will be. Don't worry."

Sidney continued to stare. "So, you're telling me that you're gonna step in for me and spar with Joey."

"Yes."

"To protect me."

"To protect your reputation," corrected Charlie.

"From her."

"Yes."

"From a girl."

"I believe she is a girl, yes."

Sidney stood and stared in silence for about another minute, then he said, very calmly, "Listen, Charlie. You go near that girl over there, and I'll pop you like a big fat balloon, and I'll keep on popping you until all the air's out. You hear me?"

Charlie sighed and shook his head. "I knew you'd try to get tough with me."

"Did you?"

"Oh, yes."

"Then why are you doing it?"

"Because you're my friend."

"No, I'm not."

"Okay. Because I don't want to see you get hurt."

"Sure you do."

"All right then. Because you're a smart guy, and you'll figure out what I'm doing."

"Which is what?"

"Which is trying to get out of sparring with you by going to spar with her, when really what I want is to get out of sparring with her, so I can spar with you."

"What?"

"I don't want to spar with her, all right? I don't want Sensei to say, 'Charlie, take your big mouth over there and spar with Joey.' I don't want that to happen because I saw what she did to you with one little half-kick to your head, so I'm trying to do something —"

"Wait, wait, wait, wait, wait," said Sidney, holding his hand up in front of Charlie's face. "Wait."

"For what?"

"What did you just say there?"

"Where?"

"About a half-kick?"

"Oh, yes. I was talking about that kick of hers that laid you out on the floor here. She pulled back on it. She kicked you at, like, half-speed."

"She what?"

"She kicked you at half-speed. She let up. She started strong and when she saw you flinch and cover up, she just finished off the motion. She was hardly trying."

"When she saw me *flinch*?" said Sidney. He had never been accused of *flinching* in his life.

"Flinch. Cover up. Cower. Whatever," said Charlie. "Whatever you want to call it. When she saw you doing it, she let up. It was like a man kicking a boy, and she couldn't go through with it."

Sidney's nostrils began to flare with emotion. "Listen. I don't know what you're trying to do here."

"I'm just trying to be helpful. Just like I said."

"You're calling a twelve-year-old girl a man. You're calling me a coward. You're saying you don't want to spar with me and you do want to spar with me."

"I'm saying I'd spar with you any day instead of her. That's what I'm saying. She terrifies me. You scare me. She terrifies me. There's a significant difference."

Sidney looked away for a moment, as if to collect his thoughts. Then he came back to Charlie. "She did not let up on that kick."

"Sure she did."

"No, she didn't."

"Sure she did."

"No, she didn't."

"How would you know? Your eyes were closed. You covered your face and your eyes were closed. But we all saw it. We saw her let up."

"No, she didn't."

"Well," said Charlie, hesitating for dramatic

effect. "It's all everyone was talking about the next day at school. That's all I know."

Sidney's face took on a different expression when he heard that. "How did they find out?" he said. "Joey doesn't even go to our school."

Charlie shrugged his shoulders. "I don't know. Willie goes home after class and phones his dad. His dad says, How'd it go? Willie tells him. His dad says, How about those three boys I sent you? How'd they do? Willie gives him some specifics. His dad gets a big kick out of the Big Kick story. He goes into school the next day and tells a few teachers in the staff room about it. They get a big kick out of it. They mention it to a few students in the hallway. You know, their little helpers. The little goodie-goodies. They tell their little buddies about it. These things get around, my friend. Gossip is a virus for which there is no cure."

Sidney stood silent. He looked stressed out by everything Charlie was telling him.

"I only heard some people talking about it at the end of the day at the bike racks," said Charlie.

"Who?"

"You know. The usual crowd over there. Matt Thompson and all those guys."

At the mention of the name Matt Thompson, Sidney closed his eyes and took in a very deep breath. This was almost too much for him to take. Then he opened his eyes and said, "Okay, Charlie. I don't know how much of what you're telling me is actually true. Coming from you, probably none of it. But I am going to spar with Joey tonight for two reasons: One, all that garbage you just said, if it's not true yet, it might become true if I don't do something about it; and two, I'm going to find out if she let up on that kick or not."

Charlie waited for a moment, then he reached out and patted Sidney on the shoulder. "I support your decision."

"Get your hand off me," said Sidney.

"These things don't come easy, I know."

"And go back over there. You've wasted enough of my time."

"Walk in peace, my friend. It's the only way."

"And stop calling me your friend."

"As you wish, comrade," said Charlie. And he turned and left Sidney alone.

6. What Sensei Duncan had them do in class was not really sparring. It was a conditioning drill called *kote kitae*, or arm rubbing and pounding. It is an exercise designed to toughen the arms, particularly the forearms, of karate students.

The steps to it are relatively easy: standing just further than an arm's length away, so that no actual fist-to-body contact is made, one partner steps forward and throws a karate-style punch; the other partner blocks the punch with a circle block, then gives the attacker a stiff karate chop to the offending arm anywhere between the fist and elbow.

When done properly, the movements of *kote kitae* are continuous: punchblockchop, punchblockchop, punchblockchop, punchblockchop, back and forth, back and forth, each student taking a turn at punching and blocking, in rotation, again and again and again, until both forearms on both students are a sore, scalding red.

Sensei Duncan knew better than to expect such a motion to come out of this first attempt at the exercise, and he really wasn't expecting anyone to be red on the arms, either, although, from his perspective, it would be good if they were. Nevertheless, this was merely intended to be an introduction to *kote kitae*, not a test.

He went over the steps of the drill several times before letting them go at it. The punch was to be aimed at chest height, never higher, and done in a specific way, as was the circle block and the chop. They were all techniques that a beginner could manage without a ton of trouble. The crispness and execution would come later with repetition and practice.

When it was time to begin, the pairings were set. Sidney stood with Joey. Charlie was matched with Mason, the tall gangly redhead. Jeffrey was told to go with Samantha, and the other two boys in the class went with each other.

Sidney and Joey got into it first.

Standing not two feet apart, they squared off. Joey stood relaxed, her hands up in the proper position, her eyes on Sidney, as Sensei Duncan said they should be. "There should be no talking through this," he had said earlier. "Keep your mouths closed. Your teeth together. That way, if you get an errant punch to the jaw, it won't hurt as much. Your eyes should be on your partner's eyes at all times. Concentrate. Focus. This is karate now. Let's get into it."

Sidney's eyes were burning. His fists were curled into tight little balls of steel. His jaw was as rigid as granite.

"What are you so wired up about?" said Joey, sensing his intensity.

Sidney said nothing.

"Okay," said Sensei, monitoring and adjusting each pairing, "throw the first punch."

Sidney exploded at the command. He lunged forward and directed a powerful blow right to the chest of Joey, catching her high in the middle of her torso, just below her neckline.

Unable to move her arms in time, much less to actually block anything, and caught completely off guard, since Sensei had said over and over again that the punch should not reach your partner's body, Joey took the full force of Sidney's punch with a mixture of shock, pain, and a searing flash of anger.

Reacting on instinct, she snapped a sizzling *shomen geri*, her toes as pointed as a railway spike, at Sidney's stomach, catching him dead center on the belly button.

Sidney doubled over in pain, his stomach burning as if scorched with a hot poker, then, all in one motion, he stood up, his face contorted in anger and agony, and lunged at Joey. But she was not standing where she had been a second ago. She had moved back a step and slightly to the right, utilizing yet another trick taught to her by her older brother: always keep your opponent off guard.

The move bought her an extra second to deal with Sidney's rage, which she used to line up and deliver another swift kick, this one to his rib cage, just beneath his left arm.

Sidney stopped lunging and grabbed another part of his body that was now badly hurting.

Joey, her own chest heaving and aching, her eyes burning like cinders, said to him between breaths, "You come at me again, I'll kick you right between the legs."

Sidney, his breathing labored by the pain in his ribs, lifted his hand and waved her off.

He was done.

The entire exchange took no more than

half a minute, and Sensei Duncan, busy with another pairing, never saw a thing.

Nor did Jeffrey, who was staring into the deep blue eyes of Samantha, trying to talk himself into stepping forward and throwing a punch.

Just when it looked like she was about to say something, he did, weakly and without much speed, but he did. He threw a punch. Samantha bapped his arm away like a child swatting a balloon at a birthday party, and chopped him across the forearm, which caused him to wince. He threw his second punch, and she did the same.

Then, she came at him. Her punches were direct and assertive. Her eyes burned with determination. Jeffrey forced her fists out of the way with more of a push than a block, and lightly tapped her arm with his hand.

They repeated the rotation one more time, then Samantha stopped and said, "Are you not hitting hard because I'm a girl?"

"What?" said Jeffrey, preoccupied with his stinging forearms.

"Are you not hitting hard because I'm a girl? Or what is your problem? Are you *sick*?"

"I *am* hitting hard," said Jeffrey, who had never thrown a punch at anyone in his entire life, and had been taught by his mother at a very young age to never argue or fight with others.

"You're throwing your punches like a sick person. Like you're some frail old lady reaching for a glass of water by the side of her bed."

Jeffrey could feel his face starting to color. This was the exact type of aggressive behavior that bothered him. "No, I'm not," he said.

"Yes, you are. And it bothers me. Because I'm standing here trying to learn karate, and you're throwing these timid little punches at me like a baby that I really don't have to block because they'd do absolutely no harm to anyone anyway."

"I'm not a baby," said Jeffrey, with anger.

"Well, you're throwing punches like a baby. Come on. We're not even really hitting each other. We're just practicing this stupid drill. Now stiffen up. Hold your arm out straight, like this. Give me something to work with."

Jeffrey could feel himself starting to burn. He stared into the annoying face of Samantha one more time, and then, in a sudden, totally unexpected burst of inspiration, he stepped forward and extended his arm with authority, his hand balled into a fist that actually felt, to him, that it could hit something and not hurt.

Samantha blocked his punch, chopped his arm and said, "That's better." He did it again with his other arm. "That's better," she said again, showing signs of encouragement.

She stepped forward and threw a punch at him. "Now knock it out of the way, like he showed us."

Jeffrey threw a circle block, then gritted his teeth and chopped down hard on her arm, hurting his hand.

"Ouch," said Samantha, grabbing her forearm. "Not that hard."

Jeffrey rubbed his sore hand. "Did that hurt you?" he said, with surprise.

"Of course it hurt me," she said angrily, rubbing her arm. "You meant it to hurt me."

"No, I didn't."

"Yes, you did."

"You told me to hit you hard," said Jeffrey, looking confused.

"I told you to give me something to work with. You didn't have to *belt* me." Samantha looked at the red mark left on her arm. "Look where you hit me."

Jeffrey gave her arm a quick glance. "That wasn't a belt. I just chopped you. Like we're supposed to do."

"It was so a belt. You even hurt your own

hand doing it." She pointed to Jeffrey's hand and sneered.

"No, it wasn't. I'm a baby, anyway, remember? How could I do anything to hurt you?" He sneered back.

"It was too a belt."

"Well, you told me to do it."

"No, I didn't."

"Yes, you did."

"Big Mr. Tough Man all of a sudden."

"I'm not a big Mr. Tough Man. You told me to hit you harder so I did."

"Try that on Joey and see what happens."

"Try that on Sidney and see what happens."

"Okay, you two," said Sensei Duncan, interrupting their battle. "Jeffrey, my dad said I'd have to use a crowbar to pry words out of you. You're talking more than anybody."

"She said I hit her too hard, and I didn't," said Jeffrey, well aware that he was behaving differently. He was feeling differently, too, all of a sudden, and he wasn't minding it at all.

"He did so," said Samantha. "First he was like Mr. Wet Noodle Boy, and then he belted me."

Sensei Duncan held his hand in the air to silence the bickering. "Another rule about karate. When you're doing an exercise with a partner, if they say you're hitting too hard, respect what they say and hit them lighter next time. Don't argue with them. If they say it's too hard, then that means it's too hard. You listen to them, and they listen to you. Now try it again."

"See?" said Samantha, giving Jeffrey a look.

"Hey, I did what you asked me to do," said Jeffrey, who could not remember ever saying Hey to anyone in his life, much less during an argument with a girl.

"Come on. Let's get back into it," said Sensei Duncan, clapping his hands together. "Let's go, you two."

Samantha and Jeffrey squared off again and Jeffrey stepped in with his first punch. His arm was stiff and strong and he felt practically nothing when Samantha gave it a block and a chop.

In fact, he smiled at her, to show it didn't hurt.

Before they had even started, Charlie told his partner, Mason, to go easy because his arms were still on the mend after falling out of the back of his dad's stupid pickup truck, but Mason still cracked at them like an ax into wood anyway.

Charlie then suggested that they start off

easy and work their way up, so they didn't aggravate any muscles before they got a chance to really do their thing, but Mason still chopped as hard the second time as he had the first.

As a final attempt to get things under control, Charlie said that the medication he was on had weakened his body to the point where harsh contact of any kind was very painful and potentially harmful, but Mason refused to bend, or even to acknowledge Charlie's words.

"Do you not understand English?" Charlie finally said, dropping his throbbing arms by his side.

Mason, who was a good three inches taller than Charlie, and had hands like a carpenter, and forearms as sturdy as wood, stared at the big boy and said nothing.

"No?" said Charlie, shaking his head. "Because I can help you with that, you know. I can tutor you in every subject, if you want. If you have a hard time understanding things. I'm a straight A student. I can give you a hand. You just have to go easy on me here. You know. I don't know how you feel about that."

"You'll tutor me?" said Mason, relaxing slightly and looking interested in what Charlie was saying.

Charlie immediately sensed an opening.

"Absolutely," he said. "I guarantee an average increase of ten percentage points in every grade I help you with. If you do everything I tell you to. And if we can work out a little something here with the karate, of course."

"Ten percentage points?" said Mason, raising his eyebrows.

Charlie nodded and smiled. "Change your life, I bet. No more hassles from your parents. Huge increase in your allowance."

Mason began doing some quick calculations in his head.

"I have references, if you're interested," said Charlie, going on.

"You said ten percentage points?" said Mason.

"My average increase is ten percent. Sometimes I go as high as twelve. A lot depends on the person I'm working with."

"Ten percentage points would put me up to 98 in Math, 94 in Language Arts, and 103 in Science," said Mason, with a smile. "How much do you charge?"

Charlie stared at him for a second. For the first time in a long time, he was speechless.

"Now throw a punch at me," said Mason, getting back into position. "Sensei said no talking."

Charlie prepared to step in with another punch. Then he said, as he quickly regained his composure, "How much homework do you have, though? I bet you have a ton."

"I don't have any," said Mason.

"How could you not have any?"

"I have a photographic memory."

"Get out."

"I do. I read something once, it's locked in forever."

"You do not."

"I do so. Ask me a question, Charles Elmore Cairns of 155 Sunset Street, postal code T5H 1S9."

Charlie stared again. For the second time in a very few seconds, he was caught without words.

"I saw your registration form for karate on Monday. See? I memorize things even if I don't want to know them. Now come on. Throw a punch at me before Sensei gets mad."

Charlie, his mind now thoroughly numb, stepped in and threw out his right hand. Mason clubbed it out of the way with his forearm, then hacked at it with a karate chop that could snap a branch off a tree.

"Focus on what you're doing and it won't hurt so much," said Mason, as he watched

Charlie cringe in agony.

"Where'd you read that?" said Charlie, his arms hurting right up to his shoulders.

"I didn't read it. I just know it," said Mason, stepping forward with a punch of his own.

Charlie knocked it away as best he could and gave Mason's arm a little chop. His hand hurt too much to hit any harder.

"Maybe I should tutor you," said Mason, with a little smile on his face.

Charlie gave him a phony smile back, then girded himself for more pain.

The class ended at 7:00 sharp. Sensei Duncan wrapped things up with front kicks, and, as a special treat, fingertip push-ups.

Charlie did not do the push-ups, citing a handful of bruised knuckles from way back that had not healed properly and therefore could not bear much weight. So, Sensei made him do twenty crunches for his belly instead.

Then everyone did their bows and picked up their things and headed out the door.

7.

Charlie and Jeffrey walked home together after class. They walked at Charlie's pace, which was much slower than Jeffrey was used to, and they stopped periodically so Charlie could sip his drink and pull whatever snacks he had from out of his bag.

Charlie was not talking much. At least, not initially. He was tired and hungry and his arms ached from the pounding they had taken.

He was angry at his mom for being unable to pick him up, and at Mason for being who he was.

"He couldn't have hit you that hard," Jeffrey said, as they crossed the field that led to the ravine, after listening to another volley of Charlie's complaints.

"Why not?" said Charlie.

"Because he wasn't supposed to. It was a

warm-up version of a warm-up drill. Besides, he was just hitting your arms. They couldn't hurt that much."

"Well, they do," said Charlie.

"Well, they shouldn't."

Charlie threw a quick look over at Jeffrey. "Who were you paired with again?" he said, growing quickly tired of being told how he was supposed to be feeling.

"Samantha," said Jeffrey, knowing what was coming.

"Oh, Samantha. Wow. I bet she can really swing the old ax when she wants to."

"Very funny," said Jeffrey, who was still feeling quite revived and invigorated with the way he had handled things in class.

"What is she, about sixty, seventy pounds with a heavy object tied around her waist?"

"My forearms are about half the size of yours," said Jeffrey. "They don't have to be hit as hard to hurt."

"And Samantha is about a tenth the size of Mason, The Talking Redwood, and that's who I had chopping away at my body parts for an hour."

"It wasn't for an hour."

"It was close to an hour."

"You're just mad because he didn't buy any of your lies."

"I told you," said Charlie, stopping to take a sip of his pop, and to emphasize his point, "they're not lies."

"Oh, yes," said Jeffrey, stopping to wait. "Your *fiction*. He wasn't buying any of your *fiction*. If you rolled all those stories of yours into a book, and somehow got someone to publish it for you, Mason wouldn't buy it. He'd take one look at it and say, 'No thank you,' and put it down. Is that better?"

Charlie started walking again. He considered what Jeffrey had said, and started to nod. "Actually, it is better. I agree with you. The stories I tell should be in print someday. And of course they won't be for everyone because what book is? But at least people like Mason will have the chance to see them."

"I never said your stories should be in print someday."

"But you agree they're stories and not lies."

"I never said that, either."

"Sure you did. Just a second ago. You said, 'I never said your stories should be in print someday.' You were saying it as a put-down, but I saw a nugget of a compliment there. You called my work stories. I thank you for that. Finally, I find someone else who believes in my work."

Jeffrey walked on and shook his head. He

was a true book lover himself, an attribute he acquired from his mother. His favorite times were browsing through bookstores with her, and lying on his bed reading the books that he brought home in his backpack from the library.

He could not imagine ever pulling one out with the name Charlie Cairns on the cover.

The two boys walked on in relative silence for a few moments, Charlie chomping on a fresh bag of potato chips, and Jeffrey replaying in his mind the sequence of events at karate. Never in his life had he squared off with anyone before, even to play-fight. Never had he talked back to anyone. And certainly never had he ever spent so much time one-on-one with a girl, not that there was anything remotely romantic about his exchanges with Samantha, but still ... it was something new.

He was enjoying these thoughts and likely could have walked the entire rest of the way home without saying another word, but Charlie broke the silence. "So my mom tells me that your family tree extends all the way up to that old gizzard who used to run the hardware store here in town."

Jeffrey shook his head again. Charlie had the tactfulness of a black bear crashing a picnic. "He's not an old gizzard. He's my grandpa."

"Oh, yes," said Charlie. "I'm sorry."

"No, you're not."

"Of course I'm not. I'm just trying to be polite."

"You should hear what he says about you," said Jeffrey.

"I can imagine."

"I bet you can't."

"I bet I can. He had the hots for my mom for a lot of years. And she stood her ground and said no every time he asked her out."

Jeffrey stopped walking and stared at Charlie.

"What did you just say?" he said.

Charlie kept walking. He waved a hand back toward Jeffrey. "It's nothing. Come on. There's no hard feelings on either side."

"What did you just say?" repeated Jeffrey in disbelief, as he started to walk again, only it was more like a march, and a very determined one at that.

"Although possibly your granddaddy is still fighting off the pangs of rejection. Mom said he took the last few times pretty hard. Granted, we are talking about thirty years ago, so the old boy should be just about over it by now."

"I don't believe what I'm hearing," said Jeffrey.

"What," said Charlie, stopping so Jeffrey could catch up, "you thought the guy just stood behind the counter all day, counting nuts and sorting screws, without ever looking up at his customers? My mother was a fine-looking woman in those days. She was slim. Wore her hair down. Not anything like she is now. I've seen pictures."

"He is married, you know," said Jeffrey, with anger in his voice.

"No," said Charlie, in mock disbelief.

"My grandma worked right beside him every day of his life."

"Not every day," said Charlie.

"Every day."

"Not at lunchtime."

"They closed the shop."

"Not on Saturdays."

"They weren't open."

"Not when he was at the back helping customers and she was up at the front guarding the till."

"You're lying again, aren't you?" said Jeffrey, finally seeing the light.

"Hey. I take offense to that," said Charlie.

"You don't take offense to anything."

"I was merely trying to protect myself."

"From what?"

"From what you were going to say about my family. I have feelings, too, you know. We all do. Everybody looks at us all the time and sees a bunch of fat, happy people, but we hurt. We have insides. We feel things."

"Like what, hunger pains?" said Jeffrey.

Charlie started to laugh. "You're a funny guy, you know that?"

Jeffrey took the compliment, but he was still not in the mood to laugh. Then he reconsidered. "My grandpa and your mom," he said, shaking his head. "To think I actually believed you for a second."

"He called us a bunch of bigmouths, or something like that, didn't he?" said Charlie.

"Something like that. It was my grandma, actually. She said your mom had the biggest mouth in Emville."

"That's not so bad," said Charlie.

"She called Sidney's mom a thief."

"A thief?"

"She swiped money from the store about twenty years ago. Her and her friends took some out of the till."

"Twenty years ago?"

"Twenty-three, to be exact."

"Wow. That's quite the memory they have. I thought things started to fade at a certain age."

"Not if it has to do with money," said Jeffrey.

"And Sidney's mom took it. Go figure."

"That's what they say. They couldn't prove anything. But they're pretty sure she was the one."

"Now that's a woman your grandfather should be hooking up with."

Jeffrey gave Charlie a look. "Would you get off that?"

"Sidney Martin's mother is a very attractive young woman. She's absolutely nuts in the head, much like her son, but she's very appealing to look at."

"I'll mention that to him when I get home," said Jeffrey.

The two boys followed the path out of the ravine and walked along the sidewalk of a new subdivision. Beyond it was the older part of town, where the trees were tall and the backyards enormous. That is where Charlie and his family lived.

"Where is your home, anyway?" said Charlie.

"I live in the one and only home my grandmother has ever lived in," said Jeffrey. "She was born in it, raised in it, and when she married my grandpa, they lived in it with the rest of my grandma's family until they could build a house of their own, but before they could move out, my grandma's father had a heart attack, so my grandparents ended up staying in it."

"And now you're living there," said Charlie, as if to suggest the continuation of a trend.

"Temporarily," said Jeffrey. "When Mom gets a full-time job again, we're moving back into the city."

Charlie thought for a moment as he and Jeffrey walked on down the sidewalk. He was about to ask about Jeffrey's parents, but he decided not to. He was just starting to get to know his new friend. He did not want to seem overly pushy or rude.

Then, he changed his mind.

"So, how long have your parents been divorced?" he said.

Jeffrey answered while staring at the sidewalk. "About four months now. They're not really divorced. They're separated."

"Who separated from who?"

Jeffrey hesitated before answering. This was not his favorite topic of discussion. "My dad left."

"Was he thrown out, or was it his idea?"

Jeffrey gave Charlie another look. "Are you sure this is your business?"

Charlie shrugged his shoulders. "I'm just

showing an interest. You don't have to answer if you don't want."

"He left," said Jeffrey, after a moment.

"Was there someone else? Another woman? Another *person*?"

Jeffrey shook his head. "Don't push it, okay, Charlie? It's still pretty fresh in my head."

"All right, all right," said Charlie, backing away. "I can always figure it out for myself."

"No, don't," said Jeffrey, stopping suddenly and raising his voice. "I don't want you thinking about my dad or my mom and why they separated or why they're not together. This isn't a joke, Charlie. Just leave them out of your head, all right?"

"Okay," said Charlie, sincerely this time. He knew he had gone too far, and was already regretting it.

"Just leave them alone."

They walked in silence the rest of the way until Jeffrey said, "I go over here," and pointed down a street lined with tall old houses and comfortable bungalows. It was not far from where Charlie lived.

Charlie stopped walking and tried to quickly come up with an apology but couldn't find the right words to get it out. Apologies were not his specialty.

"I'll see you tomorrow then," said Jeffrey, moving on. "Or whenever."

"Sure," said Charlie, still wishing he could come up with something to say. "Keep practicing those karate chops."

"I will," said Jeffrey. He turned and smiled briefly, then continued on his way home.

Charlie watched him for a moment, then turned and did the same.

8.

Sidney was curled into a little ball on his bed when his mother came home from work Thursday night. She kicked off her shoes at the door and dropped her purse on the floor like she always did. "Sidney," she called out, "I'm home."

Tizzy Martin was a small, slight woman with brown, curly, fuzzy hair and large, deep brown eyes. She was the type of person who could smile and light up the room with her pretty face, or frown and make a picture fall off the wall.

She was coming off an extended day shift at Kelly's Roadside Attraction, the restaurant and bar on the outskirts of town where she worked as a waitress. Her day had started at 5:00 in the morning with a shower, cup of coffee, and a cigarette before leaving for work. At 4:00 in the afternoon she was asked to work the supper hour to fill in for Peg, her friend and co-waitress, whose son was suddenly sick.

So Tizzy was tired and her feet were sore as she turned on the light in the small kitchen of the third-floor apartment she shared with her son, and dropped a bag of takeout on the table.

"Did you eat?" she called out. Sidney's shoes were in the front closet, so she knew he was home. "I brought us some fish and chips."

The rest of the apartment was dark, save for a small lamp in the living room, which turned on automatically at 8:00 every night.

"I could sure go for a good foot rub to-night," she said, in a voice that was louder than usual, but by no means as loud as it could get.

There was still no response.

Tizzy walked down the short hallway off the living room and knocked on Sidney's bed-room door. Then she opened the door and turned on the light and saw her son curled up on his bed.

"Honey, I'm home," she said again.

Sidney didn't move.

"Hey," she said, her voice starting to harden. "Acknowledge me or I'll stick you one in the ribs."

Sidney knew what she was talking about.

"Hi," he said, without moving.

"What's the matter with you?" said Tizzy.

"Nothing," said Sidney.

Tizzy walked over to his bed and sat beside him and patted him on the leg. "Come on. Speak. What's the matter? I have two fresh orders of fish and chips sitting out there on the table and they're getting cold."

"I said nothing," said Sidney, shoving his mother's hand away.

Tizzy stared at him for a moment before responding. She knew something was up, obviously, for this was not typical behavior for her son, who was usually out brawling with one of the neighborhood kids, or phoning her thirty times at the restaurant to ask when she'd be home.

In his quieter moments, Sidney liked to swipe one of the romance novels she took out from the library and read it with a bowl of potato chips by his side.

"Are you sick?" she said, with concern.

"No."

"Do you have a stomach ache?"

"No."

"Does your head still hurt?"

"No."

"Do you have a fever?"

Sidney rolled onto his back and looked at her. "Can you just leave me alone?" he said. "Can you just, like, leave and turn the light off and shut the door?"

"No, I can't," said Tizzy, crossing her arms and making herself comfortable on the bed.

"You can't?"

"Okay, I won't. Not until you tell me what's wrong."

"I told you what's wrong. Nothing."

"I think you're lying."

"Well, I'm not."

"I think you are."

Sidney rolled over onto his side, then onto his back again, and sat up slightly. "Well, so what? So you think I'm lying? I'm telling you there's nothing wrong, so that's all you're gonna know about it. Nothing. There's nothing wrong. Now leave. And close the door."

"So there's something," said Tizzy, after a moment.

"What?"

"You said that's all I'm going to know about *it*. That means there's something I should know about, you're just not going to tell me. And I'm going to sit here until you change your mind."

Sidney closed his eyes. For the second time in just a few hours, he was being made to feel very confused by someone he was talking with.

"All right," he said. "So there's something you should know about that I'm not going to tell you. Bravo for figuring that out. But I'm still not going to tell you anything. So scram."

"Does it have to do with karate?" said Tizzy.

Sidney could feel the blood rush into his face. Fortunately for him, he was lying down facing the wall. "No," he said. "Why do you ask?"

"Because the last time you came home from karate you were acting strangely, and now this."

Sidney turned back toward his mother, and sat up. "How was I acting strangely the last time?"

"Well, you didn't say hi when you walked in the door. You didn't ask what movie was on the TV. You didn't get yourself anything to eat. You didn't acknowledge the books I had left on your bed."

Sidney remembered the books. There were four of them, four of his favorites, and his mom had bought them at a book sale at the library in the city. He had considered saying thank you to her, but Joey's kick to his head had still been too fresh on his mind.

"Should I go on, or is that enough?" said Tizzy.

Sidney closed his eyes and rubbed his forehead with his hand and took in a deep breath. He knew he could not put off his mom forever. Not when she was this close to the truth to begin with. "Yes, it has to do with karate," he said, with reluctance.

Tizzy stiffened on the bed. She had not been wholly supportive of the idea in the first place, agreeing to it only because it was better than seeing her son suspended so early in the school year, which Mr. Douglas had pointed to as a definite possibility, since the boy had struck a schoolteacher. "What is it?" she said.

"Nothing," said Sidney.

"Don't give me nothing," said Tizzy. She was becoming angry now. "Is there someone there giving you a hard time?"

"No."

"Is there someone there beating you up?"

"Of course not."

She thought for a moment. "Is there someone there who knows more about karate than you do, and you keep fighting with them anyway, and they keep kicking and punching you like their own personal speed bag?"

Sidney hesitated before answering. This was the question that was closest to the truth, but he still wasn't sure if he should say anything or not, although he knew that by hesitating, he had just said all that there was to say.

"Sort of," he said finally.

Tizzy's deep brown eyes started to glow as she stared at her son on his bed. "There's someone in your class teaching you the hard way?"

"You could say that," said Sidney.

"There's someone there smacking you around, and no one is helping you out with it?" Tizzy could feel her temperature starting to rise.

"I didn't ask for any help," said Sidney.

"You shouldn't have to," said Tizzy. "Now get up and have some fish and chips," she said, taming her temper for the moment. She stood up and allowed Sidney to roll off the bed. As he stood straight, he winced and cupped his hands around his belly button.

"What is it?" said Tizzy, alarmed.

"I got kicked," said Sidney, slowly standing upright.

"By what?"

"By someone who knows more about karate than I do," said Sidney, through clenched teeth because of the pain.

"Is that what it was the first time, too? Did something like this happen in the first class?"

Sidney closed his eyes. This was not a conversation he wanted to have.

"Yes," he said, then he stepped past his mother and out of his room and walked toward the kitchen.

Tizzy stood still to think for a moment and collect herself. Then she went into her bedroom and changed into a T-shirt and a pair of old gray sweatpants, and made a phone call. When she returned to the kitchen, she lit a cigarette and picked up her bag of food and a plate and went into the living room, where Sidney was sitting with the remote control in his hand and his supper in front of him on the coffee table.

Tizzy sat down beside him and looked at the television.

"Peggy's working my morning shift tomorrow," she said calmly, as if to change the subject. "I covered for her tonight so she's doing my morning."

"Good for you," said Sidney, who was still in no mood to talk.

"I have my whole morning off," she said.

Sidney turned and looked at her. "You just told me that."

"I'm going to spend it at your school."

Sidney froze where he was sitting. "What?"

"I'm going to spend it at your school," said

Tizzy again. "I'm going to have a little *chat* with your principal."

Sidney stared at his mom, who was still looking at the television. Then she turned and looked at him. "I'm going to tell him what I think of his little idea. And if he doesn't like it, I'm going to *rip* his arm out of its socket and *beat* him over the head with it."

Sidney continued to stare at his mom for a moment, then he turned his attention back to the television, where the violence was at least a safe distance away.

9.

At 9:00 the next morning, the buzzer on Mr. Duncan's phone went off. His receptionist, Ms. Watson, had something to tell him.

"Mr. Douglas?" she said, as if someone else might be sitting at his desk.

"Yes."

"There's someone here to see you."

Mr. Douglas quickly scanned his Daytimer and saw that no appointments had been scheduled. "Who is it?" he said, looking at the pile of paperwork on his desk.

"They told me they don't want me to say."

Mr. Duncan closed his eyes and sighed loudly. As a school principal, he should be above these silly surprise visits from anonymous guests. But he knew better than to turn them away. For who knew who could be out there? The superintendent springing a surprise on him? A trustee with an armload of bones to pick? An angry students' committee demanding longer lunch hours and better service in the cafeteria?

"Send whoever it is in," he said, and rose from behind his desk and went and opened his door.

Before him stood an old man in a black and blue lumberjack jacket, with wispy white hair that looked like fluffs of cotton stuck to his head with glue.

Mr. Duncan reacted as if he was staring into the face of a ghost. "Mr. Anderson?" he said, the shock in his eyes coming through in his voice.

"You were expecting someone else?" the old man said, staring sternly at the principal.

"Why, no," said Mr. Duncan. "I mean, yes. No. I don't know. I wasn't really expecting anyone."

"Didn't you get my call?"

"Your call?"

"Maybe I forgot to make it," said Mr. Anderson, pausing to reflect for a moment.

It gave Mr. Duncan a chance to recuperate. "Well," he said with a polite smile, as his heartbeat began to slow, "it doesn't matter now, does it?"

"I'm sure I phoned somebody."

"Why don't you come in. Take off your coat."

"That's what I'm here for," said the old man.

"Can I get you anything? Coffee? Tea?"

"Not unless you want to have our little meeting in the bathroom," said Mr. Anderson, as he walked into the office.

He was a long, lean man, standing at least six feet tall and weighing not much more than a rake and a bucket of screws. His face was lined with weather and age. He had a hearing aid wedged into one of his ears, and he walked with a slight stoop.

He found himself a chair and sat down. Mr. Duncan closed the door and sat in a chair just to the right of Mr. Anderson instead of the one behind his desk.

"So, what gives me the pleasure?" said the principal, as if he didn't know.

"The what?"

"The pleasure. The pleasure of seeing you here today. What can I do for you? What brought you here?"

Mr. Anderson eyed Mr. Duncan for a moment. "You're the same kid who used to come into my store, aren't you?"

Mr. Duncan smiled. "I remember going into

your store several times as a young boy with my mother."

"You were the crybaby."

Mr. Duncan held on to his smile. "I believe there was one time when I had a little accident there with a saw blade. Cut me right here on my finger. I was nine years old at the time. And yes, I did cry, which was fine by me then and fine by me now."

Mr. Anderson nodded slowly, and held his stare. "I remember you always wanting a candy stick," he said finally.

Mr. Duncan thought for a moment. "Oh, yes. You had a container right there on the counter, didn't you?"

"That's right."

"I remember those now. Root Beer and Licorice. Those were my two favorites."

"You used to kick up quite a storm for your poor mother."

"Well, what child wouldn't?" said Mr. Duncan. "Big candy jar right there, head-high. Right in my face."

"My Edna used to say if you were her child, she'd stick you right in the jar and seal the lid tight," said Mr. Anderson.

Mr. Duncan continued to smile, in spite of his memories of Mrs. Anderson. "Dear Mrs.

Anderson," he said. "Always by your side at the counter. Always with something pleasant to say to all your customers."

"She was watching for thieves," said Mr. Anderson.

"Yes. Well, that too, I suppose."

"She was the one who reminded me who you were."

"Is that right."

"She said at least you could catch a thief and throw him in jail."

"That's true."

"There was nothing you could do with a crybaby."

Mr. Duncan smiled and nodded and tried to come up with something to say, but, knowing it would change nothing and only prolong their conversation, he decided to change the subject instead. "So, what was it that brought you here today again? I can't recall you telling me."

Mr. Anderson resettled himself in his chair. "You sent my grandson to some kind of class to toughen him up."

"Oh, yes. Well, that wasn't the exact reason, but I did suggest that he attend a few karate classes. Taught by my son, William, actually. Has he been to one yet?"

"He slipped out last night and went."

"Oh, good. And how did he like it?"

"He seemed to like it quite fine."

"Wonderful."

"But I told him then and I'm telling you now, Dougie Duncan is not going to tell my grandson what to do."

Mr. Duncan reflected on that for a moment, as he had done once before. He could take offense to the comment. He could get into a long argument/discussion on the role of the school/principal in the lives of students. But would it do any good? Mr. Duncan almost shook his head right in front of the old man. No, he thought to himself, it would definitely not do any good.

So he decided to take a different approach.

"Would it be better if you were the one to tell him to take the course?"

Mr. Anderson stared for a moment, and said nothing. Then he closed his eyes slightly, almost like a squint, as if he was entering a new level of deep thought and concentration. "How so?"

"Well, if you agree that the classes would be good for Jeffrey, then you can be the one to encourage him to keep going."

"And keep you out of it completely?"

"If you wish."

Mr. Anderson thought some more. "What about those kids he's with? That kid with the fat mouth and the other kid? His mother stole money from us, you know. When my Edna found out that boy was running around with Jeffrey, she nearly had a heart attack. She had to sit right down and have a drink of water."

Mr. Duncan nodded, as if he understood. "Yes, well, you know, sir, there are other kids in the class besides Sidney Martin and Charlie Cairns. And, as I said to Jeffrey once before, he does not have to become friends with those people, he just happens to be attending a class with them. It's no different than if they were all in Mathematics together, or Social Studies, or Drama."

"No grandson of mine is going to take drama," said Mr. Anderson.

"I'm just using it as an example," said Mr. Duncan. "I'm not suggesting anything by it, although I do think a little creative outlet is a good thing."

"A what?"

"A creative outlet. I think it's a good thing to have other ways of expressing yourself."

Mr. Anderson stared again at the principal for a moment, as if to figure out where the man was coming from, and thought some more. After a moment or so of that, he slowly rose up from out of his chair and pulled a small cap from his hip pocket and put it on his head.

"All right then," he said, wobbling slightly as he managed his balance. "We'll do it that way. You're out. I'm in. Karate it is. And if he comes home with one of those two boys by his side, I'll take them into the house and give them a good tanning with the first thing I can get my hands on."

Mr. Duncan smiled at the thought. "You'll get yourself arrested doing that."

"If it's that fat kid, it'll be worth it," said the old man, as he turned to leave.

Mr. Duncan hurried past him and opened the door. "Well, it was certainly nice to see you again, Mr. Anderson."

"I bet it was."

"Come again. Any time."

"No, thank you. Once here is enough for me. The next time will be Edna's turn."

Mr. Duncan blanched slightly when he heard that. Then, after his visitor was gone, he told Ms. Watson to kindly hold all of his calls, and to keep his office clear for the rest of the day of anyone wishing to see him.

Then, he closed his door.

A few minutes later, Tizzy Martin walked in. She did not knock or call out or open the door slightly and poke her nose in. She just walked in, as if it was her office, and not some-one else's.

Ms. Watson was a few steps behind her, waving a hand frantically in the air to get Mr. Duncan's attention, which she already had. "I just stepped away for a moment to get some White-out and this woman walked right past my desk and straight into your office," she said, in a voice that was close to crying.

Mr. Duncan sat at his desk and stared at Tizzy for a moment, saw the look on her face and decided to take the safest route possible. "Ms. Martin," he said, with another smile, ris-ing to his feet. "It's nice to see you again. Please, have a seat."

Tizzy sat down in the chair just vacated by old Sam Anderson.

"Can I get you anything?"

"No," said Tizzy.

Mr. Duncan then dismissed Ms. Watson, who was still very distressed, and sat down at his desk. "So, what gives me the pleasure?" he said, for the second time that morning.

"The what?"

"The pleasure. What brings you here today? What can I do for you?"

Tizzy leveled Mr. Duncan with a look that could peel paint and said, "What is the idea of setting up my son with a group of hired assassins?"

"Excuse me?"

"I said, what is the idea of setting up my son with a group of hired assassins?"

"I don't understand."

"This class you've sent him to."

"Yes."

"Two times my Sidney has gone, and two times he's come home sick and sore. The first time he had headaches. The second time he could barely stand up, his stomach hurt so bad."

Mr. Duncan looked stunned. "I had no idea."

"Now are you gonna tell me what kind of a set-up this is, or do I have to go to the superintendent?"

Mr. Duncan took a second before answering.

"I know nothing about this," he said. "I talk to my son after each class and he tells me everything is going fine, that all the kids seem to be getting along and enjoying themselves. Sure, there's the odd little moment here and there, but Willie has never said anything about your son taking a beating in any way."

"So, he's in on it too, then," said Tizzy.

"In on what?" said Mr. Duncan.

"In on whatever this *thing* is that you have my son in."

"He's not in a *thing*. I've signed him up for a karate class. It isn't a secret club we've sent him to. It's a registered school with over fifty kids in it who come here to this gymnasium in this school two and three and four times a week. The doors are always open. You can pop in for yourself and see what's going on."

Tizzy considered that for a moment. "So why is my son getting beat up, then? Nobody beats up Sidney. He's fought with grown men who haven't been able to hurt him this much."

Mr. Duncan fumbled for a reason. "I have no clue," he finally said.

Tizzy leaned forward in her chair. "Well, Mr. Principal, you better find a clue, and you better tell me what it is, or I'm going over your head. I'll call every trustee on the school board. I'll call the newspaper."

"Now, there's no need for that."

"I'll call the television networks."

"Ms. Martin. Please. Get a grip on yourself. There's no need for any of that."

"And don't you start telling me what to

do," said Tizzy, pointing a finger at Mr. Duncan and raising her voice even more.

"Of course not," said Mr. Duncan.

"When my son comes home feeling sore enough to feel sick, there's something going on."

"I can appreciate your concern."

"And I don't need you to tell me to settle down."

"Of course you don't."

"I'll settle down when I'm ready to."

"Absolutely."

"On my own. When I have the answers I'm looking for."

"I don't blame you."

Tizzy hesitated. "You don't *blame* me?"

"That's right."

"For what?"

"For feeling so upset."

"Why *should* I be blamed for feeling so upset? My son comes home and curls up in the fetal position on his bed, and I'm supposed to be blamed for something?"

"I said I don't blame you," said Mr. Duncan.

"Well, how could you even be thinking about blaming me for something? I had nothing to do with this."

"I'm not," said Mr. Duncan.

"Oh, you're not?"

"That's right."

"Oh, well. And am I supposed to be feeling *glad* about that? Should I be saying thank you for agreeing with me that I have a right to be upset?"

"Not at all," said Mr. Duncan.

"Not at all what?"

"Not at all should you be feeling thankful that I agree with you about you having a right to feel upset."

"Oh, is that it."

"I believe that's what it is, yes."

Tizzy paused for a moment. "Well, thank you so much for your support."

"You're welcome."

"That really means a lot to hear that."

"I hope it does."

Tizzy picked up her purse and prepared to leave. "But I'm still going to call the newspapers, the television networks, the board of trustees, and your superintendent if this happens one more time."

Mr. Duncan briefly closed his eyes and took in a deep breath. "I really doubt that will be necessary."

Tizzy stood up and leveled him with another glare. "Well, fortunately, it's not your decision to make."

"That's true."

"*I'm* the one who's going to decide if it's necessary or not, and *I'm* the one who's going to call them."

"I understand."

"And you can share that with your son, too."

"Share what with my son?"

"That if Sidney comes home sick and sore and unable to function again, there's going to be trouble."

Mr. Duncan nodded. "I will talk with my son about all of this."

"Good," said Tizzy. She turned and left the office. Mr. Duncan leaned back in his chair and closed his eyes and thought about how many Tylenol he should take for his headache, then someone walked into his office again.

He opened his eyes.

"By the way, was that old guy I saw leaving your office before I came in the same old codger who used to run that shabby little hardware store here in town?" said Tizzy, standing in the doorway.

"Yes, it was," said Mr. Duncan, relieved that she had at least changed the subject.

"I thought he died a long time ago."

"Apparently not."

Tizzy thought for a moment.

"I used to steal money from them all the time."

"Really."

"He didn't mention anything about that, did he?"

"I don't believe so," said Mr. Duncan, with a thin smile.

"Good." She turned to leave again, then stopped and asked him something else. "What about his wife, is she still around?"

"I'm not sure."

"That old biddy. That's the one person in the world who scared me more than I scare myself."

"I remember Mrs. Anderson," said Mr. Duncan, with a slight, knowing nod.

"I hope I never run into her again, if she is alive."

"It's probably very unlikely," said Mr. Duncan.

"I hope so," said Tizzy, and she turned and left again, this time for good.

10.

The next five weeks' worth of classes went by without fuss, injury, or complaint.

Willie Duncan introduced his students to their first *kata*, a pre-arranged series of moves and techniques that they had to learn before advancing to the next level, and took the attention away from hand-to-hand combat, if you could call it that.

They also worked on *jumbi undo*, warm-up exercises, and *hojo undo*, exercises such as *sokuto geri* and *shomen geri*, side snap kicks and front kicks, as well as *mawashi tsuki*, hook punches, and *shomen tsuki*, reverse punches.

The students responded well. They worked with reasonable diligence and focus on their *katas*, and gradually, as the two classes every week passed onto the next, they began to make progress.

However, as in classrooms of any kind, some of the students made more progress than others.

With Jeffrey, for example, karate was becoming his way out of the shy, sheltered world he had been living in, and he was loving every minute of it. After getting the first class out of the way, and all of the apprehensions and fears and doubts that went with it, he quite bravely strode into his second class, and his third and fourth and fifth and sixth and seventh, and found himself filling up with a level of self-confidence that he had never, ever, *ever* had before.

He deserved it, too. He was among the leaders in the class when it came to learning the *kata*. His circle blocks were becoming round and smooth and his footwork was second to none, due largely to the practicing he did on the hardwood floor in his bedroom.

He was developing a friendship of sorts with Charlie and he was talking more with the other kids in the class.

He'd shared a giggle with Samantha the week before when the two of them were practicing together.

It was a very gradual bit of development, however, meaning no one at school was noticing anything different about him. On the inside, he was definitely feeling stronger and more capable than ever before, but on the outside, to the people who ignored him in the hallways and made fun of him in the classroom, he was still the same little pipsqueak he'd always been, except for one thing: he did not turn pink quite as often as he used to.

For Sidney, the karate classes were having quite a different effect. For the first time in his life, sheer rage and roaring anger were not working in his favor. Instead, they were getting him hurt, embarrassed, and enormously frustrated.

To boot, he was being forced to participate in a lie to his mom that, if she ever found out about it, would lead to big and very serious trouble.

It had started the other day, after karate, as the two of them sat down to a late supper of hot dogs and tomato soup.

"So tell me about this boy who was beating you up," said Tizzy casually, as she squirted mustard onto her hot dog bun. "Is he bigger than you or what?"

Sidney said nothing for a moment, but he knew immediately that he had to be careful: To his mother, there was no greater sign of disrespect than to lie to someone, and no quicker way to send her through the roof than to lie to her.

But at the same time, Tizzy was very proud of the toughness she had passed on to her son. She had kicked Sidney's father out of their lives with her own two feet (and hands), and she had done the same to more than a few men since.

She had a reputation for being someone not to tangle with, and she wore it like a badge everywhere she went.

So Sidney was reluctant to tell her that the person beating him up was a thin, smiley-faced young girl with freckles running across her nose and braces holding her teeth in place.

"I don't want to talk about it," he mumbled, his head bowed low over his soup.

"What?" said his mom.

"I don't want to talk about it."

"How come? We've talked about this stuff before. Remember last year when that boy at summer camp jumped you from behind? We talked about that and sorted out a way for you to get him back. And you did. Remember that?"

Sidney said nothing. He continued to eat his soup.

"So what's so different about this time? So some big lug kicks you around for a while. He's not doing it anymore, and besides, you're in karate. You're gonna learn how to do it back to him."

Sidney cleared his throat, but he could think of nothing to say that would not implicate him down the road.

Across from him, his mother waited for an answer, then sighed impatiently and took another bite of her hot dog. "Well, what's his name at least? Can you tell me that, so I won't have to keep referring to him as that-boy-who-beat-you-up?"

Sidney looked up from his soup. This one he could answer. "Joey," he said clearly.

"Joey," confirmed Tizzy.

"Yes. Joey."

"Sounds like a happy little name. Does he go to your school?"

"No."

"Have you seen him around before?"

"No."

"Is he bigger than you?"

"Not really."

"He's obviously pretty tough."

"Yes."

Sidney could not bring himself to say the word "he." As it was, he was walking a very fine line between not telling his mom the truth, and lying to her. If he called Joey a "he," he would, in his own mind, at least, cross that line.

"So, what made him so tough?"

Sidney cleared his throat again. "I don't know," he said. "I got kicked once in the head and once in the stomach, that's all I know."

"Did he beat up anyone else?"

"No."

"Just you."

"Yes."

"Were you protecting someone?"

"No."

Tizzy stared at her son for a moment. "This is very peculiar, you know. Usually you're in here blabbing away about what this kid did to you and what you did to him back and what started it all."

Sidney kept his head down over his soup bowl.

"So, why aren't you doing that this time?"

He shrugged his shoulders. "I don't know."

"I know why," said Tizzy after a moment, with a little smile on her face.

Sidney looked up from his meal. His heart was suddenly beating a hole through his shirt.

"You want me to tell you?" she said. The smile was getting bigger.

Sidney gulped. He didn't know what to say.

"Your big mouth finally got you into something you couldn't get out of, didn't it?"

Sidney began to relax. His mother stared at him, smiling.

"That's it, isn't it?" she said. "You shot your mouth off to this Joey person, probably gave him a little kick when you weren't supposed to, or a punch, and he said to himself, 'All right, I'm gonna teach this kid a lesson,' and he belted you. And you didn't get the message because you were too busy being mad, so at the next class, you went after him again, and kapow, he nailed you again. Am I warm?"

Sidney didn't respond.

"Am I getting warm?"

Finally Sidney spoke.

"You're warm," he said evenly.

Tizzy burst out laughing. "You bet I'm warm. I bet I'm hot enough to roast a marshmallow on my fingertip. That's how hot I am. I'm right on the money."

Sidney smiled but said nothing.

"Well, good for him, then," said Tizzy.

"Good for Joey. He taught you a lesson I never could."

Sidney stopped smiling. "What lesson's that?"

"The lesson that you can't go on solving all your problems with your fists. And don't tell me you haven't learned it. You haven't been in a fight for over a month."

Sidney thought about that for a second, then he started in on his hot dog.

For Charlie, karate was an endurance test, a marathon with buckets of sand strapped across his shoulders and lead weights attached to his feet. It was torture. It was agony. And, he firmly believed, it was killing him. Literally, with all the striking and kicking and talk of violence, karate was killing him.

Or so he told his mother, but she didn't buy it.

"It's killing you because they don't allow you to eat during class time," she said. "It's agony because you've never done anything physical in your life. It's torture because no one listens to you yap. And it's an endurance test because you signed up for ten weeks, and you're staying in it for ten weeks, like it or not.

Now go empty the dishwasher."

In truth, Charlie's biggest problem with karate was that it required a set of skills that was completely opposite to the ones he used, and had long ago perfected, on a daily basis. Silent concentration and focus were crucial to getting a karate maneuver right, while for Charlie, talking was the way you sorted something out – silence was the final stage of the day before sleeping. In karate, you had to listen closely and follow the directions of the instructor, while for Charlie, listening got in the way of talking, and following directions meant going where someone else wanted to take you, and he had never been a big fan of that idea. Finally, in karate, obedience to tradition and protocol was as important to its study as learning the techniques of each respective *kata*, and for Charlie, obedience was for dogs.

Worst of all, though, was that no one else in the class seemed to mind all of this stuff except him. The rest of them just did what Sensei Duncan told them to do, with the occasional exception here and there, and never questioned anything for a moment.

To Charlie, it just didn't make any sense.

But really, when he thought about it, it did. What had started out in the very first class as a loose arrangement of kids and a rookie instructor had developed into a collection of decent young karate students who watched, listened, and followed the wise teachings of a black-belt martial artist.

"*Go kuro sama deshita* (Thank you for your efforts, students)," Sensei Duncan had started to say, with a bow, at the end of each of the last four classes. "I can say that to you now, because I am truly thankful for your efforts," he'd told them recently.

"*Domo arigato gozai mashta, Sensei* (Thank you very much, Sensei)," the students said back in unison, after memorizing the words from their student handbooks.

It all made Charlie feel a little bit sick, if the truth be told. So, to make himself feel better, he rebelled by refusing to learn the Japanese version of these exchanges. Instead, he simply moved his lips to the sound of his fellow classmates, and stopped moving them when they stopped talking. He also dogged it when Willie called on them to perform *zarei*, the kneeling bow, at the end of some of the classes, and he seldom, if ever, practiced anything at home.

Charlie did not expect to achieve much with this silent rebellion, but, as a self-described rebel, he saw it as the most he could do, especially considering that he was also scared out of his mind of getting caught.

For Willie, the class was becoming a dream: an extension to the glory and pride he had basked in following his black-belt test; another step toward opening a karate school of his own; and further confirmation that he did not need his big brother's name or fame to achieve personal success of his own.

True, it had also been a tad nerve-wracking, particularly at the beginning, and a wee bit tense, following the phone call from his father regarding Tizzy Martin.

But none of that mattered anymore. In addition to earning his black belt, Willie was now well on his way to becoming an accomplished karate instructor, and for that, he was most delighted.

Then, in the second to last class of the session, a fight broke out.

It started when Jeffrey tried to show Sidney the proper way of doing a front kick, something that Sidney thought he was doing quite well on his own.

"You're not keeping your toes straight," said

Jeffrey. "See, you keep your toes pointed, like this, so when you hit your target, your toes strike like knives instead of like a soft rubber ball."

Sidney gave Jeffrey a look, and then tried it again.

The whole class had been split into pairs to work on their kicks as Sensei Duncan looked on.

"No. You did it again," said Jeffrey, shaking his head. "And pull your knee right back into your chest after you kick. You're just dropping your leg down. Don't you remember Sensei talking about this? You drop your leg down like that in a fight and the guy can grab your foot after you've kicked him. Then what are you gonna do? You're fighting some guy who has your foot in his hands. That's why you pull your foot back as quickly as you shoot it out for the actual kick."

The *shomen geri*, front kick, was the closest thing to a specialty that Jeffrey had ever had in his life, and he was very proud of it. It was another one of the moves that he practiced regularly in his bedroom, and just last week at one of the classes, Sensei Duncan had singled his out as being the best one in the group. Not the hardest, Sensei had been quick to acknowl-

edge, but the one that was the most techni-
cally sound.

"Let's see you kick, bigmouth," said Sidney.

"I'm not a bigmouth," said Jeffrey. "I just
happen to know how to do a front kick. It's
not that hard."

"Let's see it," said Sidney, his hands planted
firmly on his hips.

Jeffrey got into the ready position, his hands
up and out in front of him, as if to block a coun-
ter-attack, and delivered a kick that, from any
angle, looked perfect. Then he stood back in
the ready position and kicked again, this time
with his other foot.

"There," he said with obvious satisfaction
when he finished. "That's what I'm talking
about. Toes pointed. Foot firm. Leg straight
out. Then back in again, and down."

"That's it?" said Sidney, clearly unim-
pressed.

"What do you mean, 'That's it?'"

"That's your kick?"

"Yes, that's my kick. It could be your kick
if you practiced once in awhile."

"You couldn't knock a tin can off a
fencepost with a kick like that."

"I could so."

"That's a wimp kick."

"It is not."

"It's a baby kick."

"It's the way a front kick is supposed to be," said Jeffrey.

"No, it's not. How are you gonna hurt anybody with a kick like that?"

"It's the way Joey kicks," said Jeffrey, and Sidney went suddenly silent. His ears burned red and his nostrils flared like the snout of an angry boar, but he said nothing.

"So maybe you should practice your kicks that way, too," said Jeffrey, ending the discussion.

Later, as everyone worked on their *katas*, Sidney spun the wrong way in a turn and collided with Jeffrey, who was showing Charlie the correct way of doing a circle block.

"Ouch!" said Jeffrey, who found himself in a sandwich between the two boys.

"Well, move out of the way," said Sidney, who was still brooding over Jeffrey's crack about Joey and her kicks.

"You move out of the way," said Jeffrey defiantly. "Or learn how to do the turn properly. You're supposed to pivot on this foot and turn that way, not this way. You never turn this way. It doesn't make any sense to turn this way. You turn that way."

Sidney stared hard at Jeffrey for a moment. "You know, I liked you a lot more when you were a little pink squeeze toy that just minded your own business and left everyone else alone, instead of this pipsqueak know-it-all who goes around helping people all the time."

"I liked you a lot more when you were practicing over there," said Jeffrey, motioning to the other side of the gym.

Sidney took a step forward, bringing him to within a bead of sweat from Jeffrey's nose.

"What was that?" he said.

"Boys, boys," said Charlie, sensing trouble. "Come on. This is not the time nor the place for a squabble."

"Shut up," said Sidney.

"Sidney," said Charlie, raising a finger as if he was a schoolteacher issuing his one and only warning. "That is not the language we use in this room, young man."

Sidney looked directly at Charlie and smiled. "Then let's go outside."

Charlie wavered slightly but held his ground. "That's not what I meant."

"Oh, really?"

"Get away, Sidney," said Jeffrey. "You're interrupting us here."

"Why don't you make me get away?" said

Sidney, with the same smile.

Jeffrey said nothing. As confident as he was in karate, he knew he was no match for people like Sidney in a real fight.

"I would like it if you could show me how to get someone like me out of your face, Mr. Instructor," said Sidney. "Could you show me that, now?"

Jeffrey's face began to flush slightly.

"Or would you rather wait and do it after class?"

Jeffrey said nothing.

"I see you're turning pink again. Does that mean your super powers are leaving you? Are you no longer Jeffrey, King of Karate?"

Jeffrey glanced briefly at Sidney, then back down at the ground.

Charlie stuck his hand in between the two boys in an attempt to separate them. "Come on, guys. Let's be friends. Let's go get a banana split after. On me. Just like old times."

"We have no old times, you idiot," said Sidney. "Now move your arm out of my face before I bite it off."

"Oh, come on," said Charlie. "It would take a lot more than an ordinary set of teeth to gnaw through this pork chop."

"Move it," said Sidney, with a deadly look

in his eye.

Charlie moved his arm, and looked around the gym for Sensei Duncan.

"Now listen, squirt," said Sidney, talking again to Jeffrey. "Back off with the lessons on how to do things, all right? And don't be telling me what to do in a fight, when you've probably never been in one in your life."

Jeffrey remained silent. Sidney stared at him for another moment, then cuffed him with an open hand on the side of the head. "Wimp," he said, turning to leave.

"Thief," said Jeffrey, under his breath but loud enough for Sidney to hear.

Sidney stopped moving. "What?"

"I called you a thief," said Jeffrey, who was angered and hurt by the knock to the side of his head, but even more by the return of his pink face and paralyzing fear.

"You called me a what?" said Sidney, moving into Jeffrey's face again.

"I called you a thief, because that's what you are. Actually, you're the son of a thief. Your mom stole money from my grandparents' store."

Sidney took a second to let Jeffrey's words sink in, then he belted him in the stomach and again in the head. Charlie grabbed at Sidney, and Sidney, as promised, sunk his teeth into Charlie's arm until he could feel the skin break. Charlie shrieked in horror and yanked his arm out of Sidney's mouth. Jeffrey screamed after he was hit, then lashed out at Sidney with the fury of a small tornado, sinking his fingers and nails into Sidney's face, and squeezing for all he was worth. Joey ran over from where she had been practicing with Samantha and booted Sidney in the side, just below his ribcage. In a frenzy, Sidney flipped Jeffrey hard to the ground and grabbed Joey by the arms and squeezed her until she cried out in pain. Then Sensei Duncan, who had stepped out to take a phone call, arrived and broke up the battle.

The entire fight had taken less than a minute to complete, but in its wake was Jeffrey moaning on the floor, Charlie gaping at his throbbing arm, Joey wiping tears from her eyes, and Sidney burning with more wounds to his face and body, and wincing as the firm hand of Willie Duncan led him swiftly out of the dojo.

11.

Sidney's mother was waiting for him when he came home from class. He walked into their apartment, and she was standing right inside the door with a big, happy, and proud smile on her face, which fell like an anchor from a boat when she saw her son's swollen right eye and scratched-up cheeks.

"What the hell happened to you?" she said.

Sidney said nothing. He kicked off his shoes and unzipped his coat and said nothing.

"I said, what the hell happened to you?" she said again, her anger mounting quickly.

"I got in a fight," said Sidney.

"Let me see your face," said Tizzy, moving toward her son. She looked at his eye and the cuts on his cheeks. "What sort of a person did this to you? Was it this Joey again?"

"No."

"He didn't do it?"

"No."

"Someone *else* beat you up?"

"Three people," said Sidney.

Tizzy stepped back.

"Three people?" she said, in disbelief.

"Yes."

"Three people jumped on you and beat you up."

"Not really."

"Not really?"

"No."

"Well, tell me what really happened then."

"I picked a fight with one of them, then another guy jumped in, then someone else jumped in, then Sensei Duncan broke it up."

Tizzy was dumbfounded. "This all happened *at* karate?"

"Yes."

She stared at her son for another moment, then she closed her eyes and started to rub the back of her neck, where the anger was starting to build like water in a dam.

"So, who was the first boy?" she said, preparing to get to the bottom of her son's story.

"Can I sit down?"

"Of course."

They sat down at the small dining room

table. Tizzy went into the kitchen and wrapped a cloth around a pair of ice cubes and handed it to Sidney for his eye.

"So, who was the first boy?" she said again, as she sat down.

Sidney took a deep breath. "Jeffrey Martin."

"Who?"

"Jeffrey Martin."

"Never heard of him."

Sidney shrugged.

"Why did you pick a fight with him?"

"Because he kept trying to tell me what to do."

"And you didn't like that."

"That's right."

"So, you popped him in the nose and he tried to tear your face off."

"No."

"What happened then?"

"I called him a wimp and cuffed him on the side of the head, and he called me a son of a thief, so I started belting him. Then he tried to tear my face off."

Tizzy's eyes widened as she leaned forward in her chair. "He called you a what?"

"A son of a thief. Actually, he called me a thief first, then he corrected himself and called me a son of a thief."

"Did he say why he called you that?"

"He said you stole money from his grand-parents' store."

Blood rushed into Tizzy's head like water bursting through a sinking ship. Suddenly she knew exactly who Jeffrey Martin was.

She recovered relatively quickly.

"That was a very long time ago," she said.

Sidney shrugged his shoulders, as if he didn't care how long ago it was.

"I was just a kid. Good God. I don't even know if I was a teenager at the time."

Sidney said nothing. He rearranged the ice cubes in the cloth and put a fresh, cool side back against his eye.

"So then what happened?" said his mom, wishing to move on.

"Then Charlie Cairns tried to break us up and I bit him on the arm."

"You what?"

"I bit him on the arm."

"You bit a boy on the arm?"

"Yes."

"How hard did you bite him?"

"Pretty hard."

"Did you taste any blood?"

"No, but I think I was about to."

Tizzy looked briefly at the ceiling and took in a deep breath. "And what was his name again?"

"Charlie Cairns."

"Charlie Cairns?"

"Yes."

"Is that that fat boy with the big mouth?"

"Yes."

"And the incredibly loud mother?"

"That's the one."

Tizzy shook her head and reached into her purse for a cigarette. She lit it and took one very long drag and said, "And then what?"

"Then Joey kicked me in the ribs again, when I wasn't looking."

Tizzy took another pull off her smoke.

"You were fighting with two other boys, and Joey ran over and kicked you in the ribs."

"Yes."

"Sounds like that boy needs to be taught a lesson."

Sidney looked up and, with his one good eye, stared at his mom and said, "Joey is a girl."

Tizzy looked at her son for quite a few seconds before she said, "I beg your pardon?"

"Joey is a girl," said Sidney. "I was going to tell you, but I didn't. But you know that person who was beating me up the first few weeks of class? And the person you went to see Mr. Duncan about? And the person you were so eager to meet because you thought he had taught me such a valuable lesson? Well, that person is a girl. Her name is Joanne, but everybody calls her Joey. I'm sorry I lied to you the first time you brought it up. I didn't know how to tell you, but tonight, in light of the fact that you've just admitted to stealing from Jeffrey's grandmother, I think I can tell you that I lied without getting into too much trouble over it."

Tizzy sat back in her chair and smoked her cigarette. She did not say a word.

"She's not a real big girl, either, " said Sidney, who suddenly felt like talking forever. "She's shorter than I am. She's quite thin. She wears braces and a red sun hat. She's actually quite cute when she's not kicking the hell out of me."

Tizzy smoked on until she was finished. Then she butted her cigarette in the ashtray sitting on the table and glanced briefly at her son.

"Is that all of it?" she said.

"That's the end," said Sidney, who was, for no explainable reason, feeling much lighter and better than he had been a few minutes ago. "I was given the bum's rush out of the dojo by Sensei Duncan, and then I came home to you. That's where I am right now. You're right up to date."

Tizzy stared at her son for a moment. "The bum's rush out of the what?"

"The dojo. The gym. It's called a dojo when we're doing karate."

Tizzy nodded. "I see."

A silence fell between them.

"So, how was your night?" said Sidney, after a moment or two.

"Fabulous, up to now," said Tizzy, without enthusiasm.

"Why was it fabulous?"

Tizzy paused for a moment for a deep breath. She briefly considered not telling her son anything about her night, then thought otherwise. "Well, tonight I was named night-shift manager by Mr. Kelly," she said, with a touch of pride. "I finally got that promotion I've been waiting for."

Sidney smiled and took the ice cubes away from his face. "Congratulations."

"Thank you."

"That means a big raise, doesn't it?"

"Not a big raise. But a raise, yes."

"We should celebrate."

"I brought a cake home."

"You did?"

" It's in the kitchen."

"Well, I'll go get it and cut it up," said Sidney, rising to his feet.

Tizzy watched him leave the table and walk into the kitchen. She contemplated lighting another cigarette, and then decided against it.

12.

At the same time that Sidney and Tizzy were having their conversation, Bella Cairns sat in her home, at the kitchen table, with a coffee mug the size of a large Thermos filled with peppermint tea, and said to her son, Charlie, "Tell me that story again."

Charlie told her again what had happened at karate, and why his forearm was in a bandage.

Then his mother went over the facts one more time to get them right. "So, you stepped in to help a friend of yours who was being attacked by a little apeman named Sidney, and this little fellow bit you on the arm?"

Charlie solemnly nodded his head.

"And then, despite the pain you were in, you held on to the little apeman until that blockhead of an instructor got off the telephone and ran over to help you?"

Charlie nodded again.

"And after it was all over, your instructor said that if he could, he would give you a black belt right now for the bravery you showed helping out a buddy?"

Charlie nodded one more time, and said, "Uh-huh."

"And you expect me to believe all this?" said his mom.

Charlie stopped nodding and looked at her.

"Do you?" she said again.

"It's the truth," said Charlie honestly.

Mrs. Cairns started to rumble. First her hips, then upwards to the rest of her body and her arms and finally right up to her head. She started to roar with laughter and, true to form, it sounded like a thunderstorm. She slapped the table with her beefy hand. She laughed until tears the size of raindrops fell down her cheeks.

Charlie just sat there, stunned, and took it all in, and then, when she finally started to slow down, he said, "You don't believe me?" and that got her going again.

"Do I believe you?" she said, when she could talk again. "No. I don't believe you. I wouldn't believe you if you walked in here with your hair on fire and told me your hair was on fire.

I wouldn't believe you if I saw it happen."

"Why not?" said Charlie.

"Why not?" said his mom. She started to laugh again, not nearly as hard as the first time, or the second, but she did start to laugh again. "Why not. Let me see. Why should I not believe my son, who just might be the laziest boy on the planet, and certainly one of the meekest, when he tells me that he jumped into the middle of a fight to help out a friend, and that even after he was bitten on the arm, he stayed in the fight until help arrived? Hmmm. Nothing on the surface that I can think of. Maybe it has something to do with the fact that, in addition to being lazy, you are also probably the most *inventive* boy, to use a kind word, when it comes to telling the truth, that the world has ever seen, and that it is more likely that you cut yourself reaching up into a vending machine that tried to cheat you out of a bag of potato chips, even if that vending machine was on the back of a moving truck, than it is the way you told me. How is that for a start?"

Charlie stared at his mom in shock and said nothing.

"Should I go on? Would you like another reason? I have plenty. A whole lifetime full, if you would like to sit and listen to them."

Charlie remained quiet. His mother sipped at her tea.

"You are the boy who cried wolf come to life, my dear," said his mom. "And you are about to start paying for it."

"I'm not crying wolf," said Charlie.

His mother leaned forward into his face. "That's the whole point of the story, sonny boy. The little runt keeps crying wolf when there is no wolf, and all the villagers come running for no reason, and then when there is a wolf and he cries out, no one listens to him. No one believes him."

Charlie slumped back in his chair and shook his head and for the first time in his life regretted being who he was. Then he went upstairs to his bedroom and shut the door. He did not hear the phone ring, nor did he take in any of the conversation that followed, but he did hear his mom as she lumbered up the stairs.

She opened his door without knocking.

"That was your sensei, or soonsi, or whatever he calls himself," she said.

"Yes?" said Charlie, sitting up in his bed. He had been lying down, reading a comic book to try to make himself feel better.

"He was calling to see if your arm was okay."

Charlie could feel a warm glow of excitement starting to build inside.

"What'd you say?" he said.

"When he finished talking, I told him I had some apologizing to do."

Charlie smiled for all the world to see.

"What'd he say?"

"He said he probably wouldn't have believed you either, if he hadn't been there to see it. But you were definitely in there helping your friend Jeffrey, and you definitely had your arm bit by this dogboy named Sidney."

Charlie beamed. Sweet redemption was his, and it was feeling good.

"He didn't say anything about giving you a black belt, though," said his mom.

"No?" said Charlie, the smile temporarily dropping from his face. He had forgotten about adding that part to his story.

"And he wasn't sure if you were still helping Jeffrey when he arrived, or jumping up and down screaming because your arm was so sore."

"It happened pretty fast," said Charlie. "There were people all over the place."

"I'm sure there were," said his mom.

"I was right in the middle of it, though."

"As always," said his mom. She smiled at him. ""I'm proud of you, you know, sticking up for a friend like that."

Charlie looked down for a moment, and blushed slightly.

"It was nothing," he said.

"Is that the truth?" said his mom.

"Not really."

"You shouldn't lie so much, Charlie. You really don't need to."

Charlie shrugged but said nothing. He didn't know how to respond to something like that.

His mother let it drop. "Now, come on down for a piece of cake. I picked one up from the store on my way home from work."

Charlie swung out of bed and hopped to his feet. His arm was not bothering him at all anymore.

"My son the warrior," said his mom, watching him. "Won't your father be impressed."

"Think he'll believe me?" said Charlie.

"Not a chance," said his mom. "We'll try it out on your sisters. Maybe one of them will buy it."

"Maybe Charlotte will," said Charlie, walking out of his bedroom. "She's not too bright."

His mother swatted him on the back with the tea towel she had in her hand, and followed him down the stairs to the kitchen.

13.

After he had listened to a third retelling of his grandson's story, old Sam Anderson rose to his feet and walked to the hall closet in the living room and put on his jacket and hat. Then he bent down to put his shoes on. When they were tied, he stood up straight and said to Jeffrey, who was still sitting in the living room with his mother and grandmother, "Come on, young fella. Let's get going."

Jeffrey glanced briefly at his mom. "Where to, Grandpa?" he said.

"What are you doing, Sam?" said Grandma Anderson sternly.

"I'm taking the boy to the Legion," said Sam.

"The what?" said Jeffrey's grandma.

"Oh, Dad. No," said Jeffrey's mom, Elizabeth, shaking her head.

"I'm taking the boy to the Legion and I'm buying him a beer," said Grandpa Anderson.

"Oh, for God's sake," said Jeffrey's grandma.

"No, you're not, Dad," said his mom.

"I said I'm taking the boy to the Legion to buy him a beer, and I'm taking him to the Legion to buy him a beer. Now, let's go."

Jeffrey started to stand up from the couch.

"Sit down, Jeffrey," said his mom.

Jeffrey sat down.

"Have you lost your mind, Samuel?" said Grandma Anderson.

Jeffrey's grandfather took off his hat and felt around his head with his other hand. "I don't think so. I think it's all still here."

"That's your head," said Grandma Anderson. "Just because you can feel it doesn't mean there's anything in it."

"He's only twelve years old, Dad," said Jeffrey's mother. "They're not going to serve him anything in there."

"When I tell Rudy Pontofowitch to give that boy a beer, Rudy Pontofowitch will give that boy a beer," said Grandpa Anderson.

"Rudy Pontofowitch couldn't give himself a beer if he had one in his hand and his mouth was open," said Jeffrey's grandmother.

Grandpa Anderson pointed a withered finger at his wife. "That man saved my life," he said.

"Forty-seven years ago," said Grandma Anderson.

"It's still clear as a bell up here," said Sam, tapping his head with a finger.

"Thank God something is," said Grandma Anderson.

"He's not going," said Jeffrey's mom.

"I don't even want to go, Grandpa," said Jeffrey.

"I said I'm taking him to the Legion for a beer. I'm not asking for anyone's permission. I'm taking him," said Grandpa Anderson.

"Oh, listen to this," said Grandma Anderson, shaking her head.

"He doesn't even want to go," said Jeffrey's mother.

"What?" said his grandpa, still standing by the front door.

"He doesn't even want to go."

"Says who?"

"Says Jeffrey. He just said he doesn't want to go."

"I'll go out with you, Grandpa. But not for a beer," said Jeffrey.

"What would a twelve-year-old boy want with a beer anyway?" said Grandma Anderson.

"You'd be surprised, Mom," said Elizabeth.

"How about a glass of rum, then, right here in the kitchen?" said Grandpa Anderson, looking excited at his new idea.

"No, Grandpa," said Jeffrey, shaking his head.

"Jeffrey likes ice cream, Dad. He likes potato chips."

Grandpa Anderson shook his head. "In my day, when a young man survived his first combat mission, we took him out and bought him a drink."

"Here we go again," said Grandma Anderson.

"I know, Dad," said Elizabeth. "But Jeffrey's still a little young for all that, and this wasn't really a combat mission he was on, and his survival was never really in doubt."

"He stood up for the family," said Grandpa Anderson, his voice quickly rising. "That takes honor. That's pride."

"I'll drink to that," said Jeffrey.

"Jeffrey," said his mother, giving him the eye.

"I'm going to bed," said Grandma Anderson, rising from the couch.

"I think you should be heading that way, too," said Jeffrey's mom to Jeffrey.

"You really called him a thief, didya?" said

Grandpa Anderson, with a smile on his face.

"After he hit me," said Jeffrey.

"Good boy," said his grandpa.

"I really don't condone any of this," said Elizabeth, shaking her head.

"Oh, you," said Grandma Anderson to her daughter. "Give it a rest. The boy stood up for himself. He didn't take any crap."

"Mother!"

"You should learn from him. The next time you go looking for a man, you tell him you're not standing for any crap this time. Once is enough."

"Mother. Go to bed."

"She's right," said Grandpa Anderson. "This boy taught you a lesson today."

"I don't want to hear any more," said Elizabeth firmly to her parents. Then she turned to Jeffrey. "And I do not want to hear any more of this going on at your karate class, either, or you'll be out of there faster than you know it. Do you understand?"

"Yes," said Jeffrey, bowing his head slightly. He understood his mother very well.

"Don't you go feeling bad for what you did tonight," said Grandma Anderson, pointing a finger at her grandson.

"I want him to know that what he did is

not right," said Elizabeth.

"This boy acted like a true Anderson for the first time in his life tonight," said Grandpa Anderson. "Don't you go telling him to stop it."

"I want him to stop it," said Elizabeth.

"You stopped it, that's why you want him to stop it. But he's not gonna stop it," said Grandma Anderson, her eyes on fire. "He's not gonna stop it. And I'll be the one to make sure of it."

"You're not the one raising Jeffrey, I am," said Elizabeth. "So stay out of his life."

"How can we? We're tripping over the boy's feet every time we turn around," said Grandpa Anderson.

"Do we have to remind you who actually owns this house you're living in?" said Grandma Anderson.

Jeffrey looked at his mother and gulped. He could see the emotions running wild on her face — the anger, the frustration, the pain — but she said nothing to her parents. Instead, she stood ready to explode for a moment, her face a quivering red, and then she turned away and left the room without saying a word.

Later, Jeffrey knew she would cry herself to sleep, and in the morning, she would not say a word about any of it.

But tonight would be different. He followed her upstairs and knocked on her bedroom door. He could hear her crying inside. He knocked again.

"Who is it?" she said, her voice weak from sobbing.

"It's me," said Jeffrey.

"Go to bed, Jeffrey."

"No."

"Yes."

"No."

"I've talked about it enough with you already tonight. Just go to bed."

"No."

"Jeffrey."

"What?"

"Go to bed."

"No."

"Jeffrey."

"What?"

"Stop playing around. It's after ten and you have school tomorrow. A test, as I recall, in mathematics. Now go to bed and get some rest. We'll talk about this in the morning."

"No, we won't."

"Yes, we will."

"We never do."

"Well, tomorrow we will."

"No, we won't."

"Jeffrey."

"What?"

"Go to bed."

"No."

"Oh, for God's sake."

Jeffrey heard the squeak of the bedsprings as his mother got off the bed and walked toward the door. She flung it open and looked hard at her son.

"Can you not tell that I am not in the mood for your company at the moment?"

"Yes."

"So, why are you here?"

"Because."

"Because why?"

"I wanted to say good night."

"Fine. Good night."

"And that I won't get into any fights ever again."

"Good."

"Because it's no way to resolve anything and it's a good way to get hurt."

"That's right."

"I'm much better off just turning the other cheek and walking away."

"Okay, Jeffrey. That's enough."

"Just like you and Dad were with each other."

"Go to bed now, Jeffrey."

"Whenever he'd get mad at you, you'd leave the room. Whenever you were mad at him, you'd leave the room. And finally, when the two of you got really mad at each other, he left the house. For good."

Elizabeth did not reply to her son right away. This was the first time she had ever heard his take on their marriage, and it was not a very flattering one.

"There was a little more to it than that, sweetheart."

"I'm sure there was."

"And some day you'll hear all about it."

"You mean you'll actually tell me?"

"Perhaps."

"And what should I do in the meantime? Run around hiding from everyone? Or should I actually use some of this stuff at karate that I'm learning and feeling good about?"

Elizabeth sighed deeply and leaned against the doorway of her bedroom. It was true, what her mother had said: Jeffrey was acting like an Anderson, and as much as Elizabeth deplored so much of her parents' behavior, she knew that her way hadn't been the answer either.

"Your father would be very proud of the way you stood up for yourself tonight," she said.

"How about you?"

"I'm proud of you, too," she said, with only mild reluctance. "I'm tired, and I'm an emotional wreck, and I worry every day that you're going to be all right, but I like the way you stood up to that boy."

"I'm not going to start picking fights with every kid who bumps into me in the hallway now, Mom," said Jeffrey.

"I know," she said, and she smiled at him for the first time since hearing his story, and pulled him in to give him a hug.

As she held him, she too felt like buying him a beer, and cracking one open for herself.

14.

At 9:00 the next morning, the three boys were called down to Mr. Duncan's office for a meeting.

Jeffrey and Sidney arrived first. They looked at each other briefly, but said nothing. Then Charlie walked in eating a granola bar.

"No food in the office, please, young man," said Ms. Watson.

Charlie peeled off the rest of the wrapper and slid the last half of the bar into his mouth, pushing the last bit in sideways so it would all fit in.

"That's not what I meant," said Ms. Watson.

Charlie shrugged and started to open his mouth to say sorry, but decided against it.

The three boys then sat down in Mr. Duncan's office and waited. They were silent, except for Charlie rolling the food around in his mouth as he tried to chew it.

A few minutes later, Mr. Duncan arrived.

"Good morning, gentlemen," he said briskly, as he walked in. His manner was stiff and serious and his face solemn, as if he was bearing bad news.

"Morning," said Jeffrey and Sidney, almost in unison.

"Top of the day to you, sir," said Charlie, his mouth nearly empty.

"I'm afraid you won't be here long. I heard the complete story about last night from Willie. I see no reason to dawdle over this. I have work to do, and plenty of it. I've wasted enough time with you three already."

"Can I say something, sir, before you get started?" said Charlie.

"I have started, Charlie, and no, you cannot."

"Just one thing?"

"No."

"One little thing?"

"What did I just say?" said Mr. Duncan.

"Well," said Charlie, "among other things, you said that you heard the complete story about last night from your son, Willie."

"And?" said Mr. Duncan.

"And what?"

"And what else did I say?"

Charlie took a second to think. "Well, you also said that you had plenty of work to do, and that you saw no reason to dawdle over this."

"And?" said Mr. Duncan, leaning forward in his desk.

"And that you've wasted enough time with us already."

"Yes. And?" said Mr. Duncan, growing more impatient by the moment.

"That's about it, isn't it?" said Charlie. He looked over to Sidney and Jeffrey sitting beside him. "You guys hear him say anything else?"

"He also said that he doesn't want you saying anything," said Jeffrey.

"Did he?" said Charlie.

"Yes," said Jeffrey.

"Did you?" said Charlie, looking back at Mr. Duncan.

"Yes," said Mr. Duncan.

"I don't remember that."

"Well, he did," said Jeffrey.

"Yes, I did," said Mr. Duncan.

"I thought I had heard everything," said Charlie. "Oh, well. Anyway, I just want to say one little thing."

"The three of you are suspended from school for three days," said Mr. Duncan, cutting to the quick. "When you return, you will serve two weeks of detention after school, and you will be on clean-up duty at the gymnasium for the next four weekends."

"What?" said Jeffrey, his face a mixture of pink disbelief and astonishment.

"Oh, God," said Sidney, rolling his eyes, crossing his arms and slouching in his chair all in one motion.

"I just want to say, on behalf of my mom and dad, thank you for enrolling me in your son's karate class," said Charlie.

"You had your chance," said Mr. Duncan, ignoring them all. "I gave you every opportunity to get yourselves on the right track, and you blew it. You blew it big time, and now you're going to pay for it."

"He called me a thief," said Sidney, pointing to Jeffrey.

"He hit me on the side of the head and called me a wimp," said Jeffrey.

"I don't want to hear it," said Mr. Duncan, his voice firm. "I heard all about it once already, and that was enough."

"Can we pick which days we have off?" said Charlie.

"You are suspended as of this moment and you will return to class in three days. You are expected to stay up on your studies. There will be no grace period for you when you return. And you are banned from karate."

"We're what?" said Jeffrey, looking even more stunned than he had been a second ago.

"That's right. You are banned from karate," said Mr. Duncan. "No more wasting my son's time. That's it. You're finished."

Charlie shook his head and sighed heavily. "That's a big price to pay for being a hero."

"A what?" said Sidney.

"A hero," said Charlie, turning to look at him.

"You're not a hero."

"Hey, I broke up the fight," said Charlie. "I was a totally innocent bystander, and I stuck my arm in between you guys to break it up. I put myself on the line. I took a bite on the forearm from you for it."

"That's not breaking up a fight," said Sidney.

"I broke up the rhythm of the fight," said Charlie. "Once the rhythm is gone, the fight is dead."

"You did not," said Sidney.

"Sure I did. That's what my mom wants to thank you about," said Charlie, turning back to Mr. Duncan. "She said your son's class has changed my life. I stepped in to help somebody and I had never done that before ever. Nothing even close to it. So, she says thank you for giving me the opportunity to grow. Up, not out. I grow out well enough on my own."

Mr. Duncan looked at Charlie and said nothing, but in the back of his mind, he started to think, and as he thought, he recalled Willie saying something quite similar to what Charlie's mother had apparently said: that never, not in a million years, had either one of them ever expected Charlie to get involved in someone else's battle.

"My grandpa said the same thing about me," said Jeffrey.

"He did?" said Mr. Duncan, his large eyes opening wide.

"He said it's the first time I've ever acted like a real Anderson before. And my grandma said it was good that I finally didn't take any crap. And my mom even agreed with her. Eventually."

Mr. Duncan continued to stare at Jeffrey for a few seconds after the boy stopped talking. "Any crap?" he said finally.

"That's what she said," said Jeffrey.

"Your grandma said 'crap'?" said Charlie.

"She always says 'crap'," said Jeffrey.

"That's enough," said Mr. Duncan.

"What else does she say?" said Charlie.

"I said, that's enough," said Mr. Duncan, with more force than the first time.

Charlie and Jeffrey stopped talking. Mr. Duncan went back to thinking about his decision to ban the boys from karate.

Then Sidney cleared his throat and started to speak. "My mom didn't say anything to me about last night. She was too stunned after I told her that the person beating me up all this time was a girl."

Mr. Duncan's eyebrows yanked up his forehead as if pulled on a string. He had not known about Joey before, either.

"But I told her afterwards, after we had cake, that it's no fun trying to be a tough guy all the time, and karate seems to be a pretty good place for me to chill out and relax a little bit, because no one there thinks I'm tough anymore anyway."

Charlie reached out and put his hand on Sidney's shoulder. "That's not true, Sidney," he said.

"Move your hand, Charlie," said Sidney.

"We love you just the way you are."

"Move your hand, Charlie," said Sidney again.

Charlie began to pull his hand away. "It

takes a real man to say what you just said."

"Now shut your face, Charlie," said Sidney, when Charlie's hand was clear from his shoulder.

"I respect you now more than ever."

"And don't even think of saying a word of this to anyone outside this office."

"I think I'm going to cry."

"You'll be crying, all right."

"Okay, boys," said Mr. Duncan, but that was all he said. He was too amazed to say much more than that, such was the force of the stories he was hearing.

After another minute or so of deep thought and silence, he looked over to Jeffrey. "So, your grandparents are pleased with your progress in karate?"

"I think so," said Jeffrey, with a shrug.

"And your parents would like you to continue?" said Mr. Duncan, looking at Charlie.

"Dad says fifty bucks is mine when I can smash a two-by-four with my forehead."

"And how about you?" said Mr. Duncan, looking at Sidney.

Sidney shrugged.

"I don't know how excited Mom is about the whole thing, but I know I'd like to stick with it. Until I learn how to kick, anyway."

Mr. Duncan sat back in his chair and thought for another moment. "Okay," he said, leaning forward again, "here's the deal. You are not banned from karate. But, you are on probation. One strike against any of you, and you're out. Simple as that."

The three boys started to smile.

"Your suspension for fighting still stands."

The smiles fell. Charlie raised his hand in the air.

"There's no way my mom and dad will let me go to karate and continue my successful journey into manhood if I get suspended."

"Same with me," said Jeffrey, instantly turning pink. He was not used to speaking out this way, but, in a case like this, he was willing to give it a try.

Sidney said nothing.

Mr. Duncan shook his head. "All right. You're not suspended. But detentions, after school, every day for two weeks, starting next week."

"Except Mondays and Thursdays," said Charlie.

"Why except Mondays and Thursdays?" said Mr. Duncan.

"Those are karate nights. Classes start at six. I need time to get home and eat. Relax.

Focus on my training."

Mr. Duncan stared for a moment at Charlie. "All right. Except Mondays and Thursdays."

"And Fridays, because teachers don't stay late on Fridays," said Charlie. "Everybody knows that."

"Don't push it, my friend," said Mr. Duncan.

"We can't stay in there by ourselves," said Charlie.

"Just be in the detention room next Tuesday at 3:00. We'll handle the rest from there."

"All right, sir," said Charlie.

"Now go," said Mr. Duncan.

The three boys, all smiling, filed out of his office. Mr. Duncan leaned back in his chair and rubbed his eyes and took in a few moments of silence and peace. Then, his intercom buzzed.

"Yes," he said, to Ms. Watson.

"A Sam Anderson called you earlier, sir, while you were with the three boys?"

"Yes," said Mr. Duncan, a ripple of uneasiness passing through his body.

"He wanted to know if you could meet him at the Legion for a beer."

"Pardon me?"

"He wanted to know if you could meet him at the Legion for a beer."

"For a *beer*?"

"I believe that's what he said, sir. Yes."

Mr. Duncan closed his eyes and said nothing. First the old man wanted him out of the picture, now he wanted to go out for a beer, at 9:30 in the morning.

"Tell him no," said Mr. Duncan.

"He said he'll be by at 11:00 to pick you up."

Mr. Duncan's head flopped down until his chin touched his chest.

"He said something about celebrating his grandson's first successful mission," said Ms. Watson.

Mr. Duncan nodded and said nothing. Then he lifted his finger off the intercom, putting an end to his conversation with Ms. Watson.

All he could do now was hope that when he finally got rid of the old man, Tizzy Martin wouldn't be standing behind him.

One Missing Finger

Don Trembath

All Charlie wanted to do was watch a little TV. But no, he's told to walk the dog, and walk her he does, right into a handful of trouble with a beautiful older girl, her very jealous boyfriend and an elusive pair of red gloves.

Meanwhile, Sidney's fallen for Joey even though her mother wants him to buzz off. And Jeffrey just wants his father back. But would getting his parents back together bring happiness to his life?

One Missing Finger continues the story of the three small-town misfits introduced in *Frog Face and the Three Boys*. Reaching new comedic heights as they stumble further through the jungle of friendship and into the swamp of young love, the three boys realize that as they get older, they need to rely on themselves and trust each other.

Don's teen novels, including *Lefty Carmichael Has a Fit* and the Harper Winslow series, have all gone on to become bestsellers. *Frog Face and the Three Boys* has been short-listed for the Ontario Library Association's Silver Birch Award. Don lives in Morinville, Alberta.

1-55143-194-7; $8.95 CAN/$6.95 USA

Don Trembath was born in Winnipeg, Manitoba, and moved to Alberta at the age of 14. He graduated from the University of Alberta in 1988, with a B.A. in English.

Don's first novel, *The Tuesday Cafe*, was inspired by six years of work at the Prospects Literacy Association in Edmonton. It was nominated for both the YALSA Best Books for Young Adults and the YALSA Quick Picks for Reluctant Readers lists. It also won the R. Ross Annett Award for Children's Literature and made the ALA's "Popular Paperbacks" 1997 list. The second installment in the Harper Winslow series, *A Fly Named Alfred*, was nominated for the prestigious Mr. Christie's Book Award. *A Beautiful Place on Yonge Street* was chosen as a YALSA Popular Paperbacks for Young Adults.

Lefty Carmichael Has A Fit, Don's fourth book, was nominated for the CLA Book of the Year, and has been widely praised by such journals as *Publishers Weekly*, *School Library Journal* and *Booklist*. It was also included in the Young Adult Library Services Association "Best Books for Young Adults" for the year 2001.

Don divides his time between school and library presentations and his active young family.